There Are Things I Know

KAREN B. GOLIGHTLY

Fairlight Books

First published by Fairlight Books 2018

Fairlight Books
Summertown Pavilion,
18 - 24 Middle Way,
Oxford, OX2 7LG

A CIP catalogue record for this book is available from the British Library

1 2 3 4 5 6 7 8 9 10

ISBN 978-1-912054-60-2

www.fairlightbooks.com

Printed and bound in Great Britain by Clays Ltd, Elcograf S.p.A.

Designed by Sara Wood

Illustrated by Sam Kalda
www.folioart.co.uk

This book is dedicated to the three who have my heart: Bella, Phin, and Pip. Also, to every man, woman, or child who sees the world a little differently.

Chapter 1

There are things I know, things I remember, and things that other people tell me.

I know that my momma's phone number is 373-1888. That much I know for sure. She wrote it on my arm when we went to Disneyland, Chuck E. Cheese's, That Amazing Pizza Place, and just about anywhere else she thought I might get lost. She wrote it with a Sharpie Marks-A-Lot, one of those permanent ink markers. Only they're not permanent. If you wash them enough, scrubbing them hard like Uncle Dan did, then eventually those numbers will disappear off your arm. But they didn't disappear out of my brain, because even though my brain doesn't always work right, even though the words don't always come out of my mouth like my brain tells them to, I know numbers. And my momma's numbers are 373-1888. I can see those seven numbers in my head, just how she wrote them in that black ink, the seven crossed in the middle 'like the French do,' she'd said, and the six circles of the 8s stacked on top of each other like a Lego brick. Seven numbers. The first three add up to 13. The second four make 25. Together they make 38. But every time I call home, using those numbers, I get the 'Beep, beep, beep. I'm sorry, but your call cannot be connected at this time. Please check the number and try again.' I checked the numbers, added them up, divided them by two, and I called again and again. Still the lady told me to check my numbers. Since I have to sneak to call my momma, I don't get that many chances, but I'll keep trying. I know she's out there.

I think there are three other numbers that go along with those seven, or so this kid at school told me, so sometimes I try them. Most of the time, I get the lady telling me to check my number again. Sometimes I get somebody who doesn't sound at all like my momma, and I ask them, 'Do you know my momma? Her name is Katherine Armsteaden. Her number is 373-1888.'

Normally they just pause, and say, 'You got the wrong number, kid.' And I wonder if my momma got her own number wrong. But sometimes they say, 'Are you lost, little boy? Do you need help?' I do need help, if I'm ever going to find my momma again. But those people don't seem to know how to help me. They tell me that I have the area code wrong. I'm not even sure what an area code is, but once I did call Hawaii. That was on my teacher's phone, when she gave it to me to use as a calculator in math. Like I need a calculator.

8

Uncle Dan tells me that my momma is gone, gone to heaven, and she isn't coming back. And that we live in Arkansas now, where there is a lake, green grass, and the biggest mosquitoes I've ever seen anywhere. They bite and make giant red welts on my arms and legs that itch like crazy. I try to keep count of them, but every time I go outside, more and more appear. I'm up to 77 right now.

We have chickens too, which I kind of like, but I'm kind of scared of too. The rooster is really scary, so I try to stay far away from him. I don't know where Arkansas is, but it seems really far away from my home and my momma. I also know that I have a brother and sister, Christopher and Sabrina. They are bigger than me. Christopher is seven years older than me, which makes him 15. He is supposed to be learning to drive, but it makes him sweat and breathe funny every time he does it, or at least it did when I lived there with Momma. Plus we never could listen to the radio when he was driving because it made him nervous, so he didn't drive too much. Momma said he had to, though, 'just in case something ever happened.'

She used to play this game with us called 'The Survival Game.' It was where she would set up situations where she couldn't drive or was too sick to save us. 'Then,' she would say, 'what would you do?' Her scenes were always exotic vacations that we couldn't possibly ever go on, but she described them like we were right there.

'So, we are driving along the west coast of Costa Rica. Hear the waves, smell the sea, feel the sun on your skin. We are just driving along and suddenly I feel sick. I pull over to the side of the road, and then pass out.' She looked at each of us individually. 'What do you do to save this family?'

She liked the drama of it all, I think. Sabrina shouted out, 'I'm driving us. But first Christopher would have to help me move you over.'

Christopher chimed in, 'I call shotgun.'

'You can't have shotgun. How are we supposed to get Mom all the way into the back seat if she's passed out?'

'The same way we get her into the passenger seat. Push her over.'

Sabrina scowled at him, while Momma laughed and said, 'I'm not sure I'm going to survive this one.'

Then she got serious. 'No, really. What are you going to do, Christopher? Just throw me into the back seat?'

He thought for a second. 'Sabrina and I will pick you up and walk you to the back seat, where Pepper will try to revive you.' He paused. 'Then I call shotgun, so I can navigate and be in charge of the radio. Anyway, I know more Spanish than anybody in this car, so I can read the street signs for Sabrina. *Policio, hospitalia, el speedo limito.* See? I'll save this family.'

I nodded, convinced that he would. And I would revive my momma. I would hold her hand and maybe rub a cold rag on her head so that she would wake up.

Sabrina always had to be the driver, Christopher the navigator, and they gave me foraging for food or keeping Momma company, whichever needed my attention the most. I think I could drive just as good as Sabrina if I were a little taller. I've practiced on lots of video games, and, soon, I'll be able to drive myself away from here.

Momma made up story after story, emergency after emergency. All of us out in the middle of the ocean on a boat, surrounded by sharks, and Momma was throwing up from seasickness. Or the four of us on top of a volcano, Momma fainted from the smoke, and we had to figure out how to survive. Or in a rainforest, mean monkeys attacking us, and Momma was stuck in quicksand. She came up with all kinds of situations, but she never made us plan for her dying in a car wreck while I was at That Amazing Pizza Place.

Sabrina is nine years older than me, so that makes her 17. She has fits sometimes, like I used to when I was in kindergarten and I had lost all of my words. I would yell and scream, because I couldn't make my brain work the way it was sup-posed to so that I could tell people what I wanted to say. I don't think my kindergarten teacher liked me very much. I went to the principal's office a lot that year, but she let me play with her iPhone, so that was fun most days. I'm not sure why Sabrina has fits, because she didn't lose her words like me, but sometimes she yells and screams, and one time she even hit my momma on the arm. She's not little like I was when I had my fits, so my momma can't just hold her tight and tell her that it's going to be okay. I loved it when she did that. She would whisper, 'It's going to be okay, Pepper. Breathe. Deep. In and out. In and out.' Breathing helps a lot when the world goes all shaky, and your brain turns backward and starts spinning, and you can't tell people what you want.

My momma made everything okay again in the world and made my brain turn back the way it was meant to be so that I could remember my words again. Now I don't have anybody to hold me tight like that, so that my brain slows down enough to turn itself right. I don't think that Uncle Dan knows how to do what my momma did anyway. I have to slow down my breaths on my own and even them out, or just count until I try to reach infinity, which you can't really reach, when my brain gets out of whack. Uncle Dan's not really a hugging kind of guy, which is fine by me. He's more of a fishing kind of guy. I guess I'm lucky that he saved me, when my momma went to heaven, but I wonder what happened to Sabrina and Christopher. Do they still live in my house? Do they miss me? I miss them. And my momma too. How could they survive The Survival Game if I wasn't there to help?

I was on a field trip, pretty much the only reason I even liked second grade, to That Amazing Pizza Place. My momma had to work that day, so I went with my teacher, my friend Jonah's momma, and 19 of my classmates. I liked Jonah's momma, but I wasn't so excited about the little redheaded girl in my class, Rosalind Jane, going, because she was always hugging me and asking me questions. I couldn't stand her hugging me. But my momma told me that it was nice when people hugged you. It was nice when my momma hugged me. She smelled like vanilla and had the softest skin I had ever touched. Plus she rubbed my head and sometimes my ears when things got too loud, and that always made me feel better. But I didn't like it when kids at school hugged me. They squeezed too tight. It hurt my skin. So, I stood there, stiff as a tree, and let them hug me while I cringed inside. If I focused on my heartbeat, and counted it as it pounded in my chest, it made the hugging go faster. I breathed in and out slowly, so that I could stay focused on the heartbeats. Eventually they would let go and walk away. I tried to smile at them and say, 'Thank you for the hug,' even though I didn't like it one bit. I guess that I was lying when I said thank you, but I was just trying to be polite.

That morning, in the classroom, Mrs. Walton put name tags on each of us, right over our hearts. Mine said 'Pepper,' which wasn't my real name. That was Joseph Phillip Branigan, but everybody had called me Pepper since I was a baby; that's what my momma said. I liked it, Pepper, the way the 'p's had sticks to hold up their circles, and the 'e's looped over. I sometimes worried about the 'r', who seemed to be left out on his own, hanging onto the end of my name. But I knew that nobody else had the name Pepper, and that it was, as my momma said, 'made especially for me.'

We had to ride the big yellow bus, for what seemed like forever, before we finally got to walk across the hot black pavement, with 124 yellow lines, into the doors that said 'swoosh' when you went through them.

'Stay with your partner,' Mrs. Walton said in her teacher voice.

Rosalind Jane grabbed my hand and gave me a quick squeeze. I froze. I wasn't sure I could stand her holding my hand the entire time we were there. She was one of the 'special' kids like me. We went to speech together and to a lady who tried to teach us not to write so messy. Rosalind Jane didn't eat like other kids and had a tube coming out of her stomach, where, she said, 'I eat my food.' I wasn't sure how you ate food out of a tube, but I knew that her hands were sweaty, and I couldn't stand sweaty hands. I knew I had to get away from her. But right after the cool air hit me, so did the smells of That Amazing Pizza Place: pepperoni, sausage, Dr Pepper, sweat, something chocolate, and a little bit of pee, all rolled into one. I was okay with that. But it was really loud in there. Lots of video games, air hockey, laser tag, go-carts, bumper cars, a bouncy thing, and people talking all at once. I had to put my hands over my ears, because it was too loud, so Rosalind Jane just held onto my elbow.

Mrs. Walton was trying to pay for us to get in and get us all tokens at the cash register. She gave me eleven tokens that clanked against each other in my pocket. I kept my hand there, guarding them, and hoping to keep it away from Rosalind Jane.

'Hold your coins,' I told her. 'Or they're going to get lost.'

She clapped her hands together so her tokens wouldn't disappear and looked at me surprised. I didn't really talk that much. Not because I didn't have anything to say, but because the words didn't always work out how I wanted them to. So sometimes it was easier just to talk in my head. Or count. Counting was fun.

I knew it would keep her busy, because she was a girl, and had on a dress, so she didn't have any pockets. I also knew that tokens were the key to playing all of those loud, light-up games I saw ahead on the left.

I walked with the group for a few minutes, while everyone started playing games like air hockey, Street Fighter, Pac-Man, and some motorcycle driving game that looked pretty fun. I looked around. It was still loud, but I was getting used to it, little by little. There were workers wearing blue shirts and blue baseball caps, with name tags like us, running all over the place. You would think they had never seen kids before. Most of them looked like teenagers, like Sabrina's friends, with their ears pierced, one, two, three, even four, times, and their cell phones stuck in their back pockets, ready to text at any moment.

One guy wasn't running around at all, though. He had a blue baseball cap and a blue shirt on, but didn't have a name tag like the other workers did. And he wasn't a teenager. He was older, like my mom's age. He was hanging around the claw game, kind of watching everybody, probably making sure that nobody spilled their drinks on the video games. He smiled at me for a second, but I looked away. I don't like looking at people in the face. It's too hard to put the pieces together quick enough to make the full face picture.

Then I saw one of those blue tunnel things, and I knew where it would be quiet enough for me. I looked up at the roof. I tracked the tunnel all the way across the room, seven separate sections, with forty-eight joints, three slides, six climb down ladders, and a ball bin at the end. And only eight windows in the whole thing. That looked cool. I checked out Mrs. Walton, then Jonah's momma, and finally Rosalind Jane. They were all busy at the Skee-Ball machines, so I edged quietly toward the tunnel entrance. I was really good at disappearing. I was quiet, so no one really noticed. I put on my ninja quiet moves and slowly inched toward the tunnel. If I tiptoed really slow, then people wouldn't even see me.

The blue plastic was cool against my knees as I crawled through, shutting out the beeps, dings, bangs, and kids screaming behind me. The further I crawled in, the more quiet it became, and the plastic wrapped around me like a blanket, shutting out the loud, loud world outside. I crawled up a ladder, then forward for a few minutes. I stopped at the first window and looked down. My classmates looked like ants down there, all running around in a hurry. I wasn't sure what they were in such a hurry to get to, but I was glad I was up here away from it. Some kid, who smelled like peanut butter, came crawling by me.

'What're you doing?' he asked.

I just ignored him and went on toward the next joint. I could see six joints in this section, so I knew I had a lot more tubing to cover before I came to the ball pit at the end. I would stop every now and then, I wasn't in any kind of hurry, and run my hand along the smooth plastic tunnel. I always wondered how they made these things. They were so smooth, no bumps or anything. I would have to try to Google that and find out. I wasn't so crazy about the way it smelled, like sweat and the kids at school, half of their lunches smeared across their shirts. But it shut out most of the noise from below, so, for me, it was one, two, three, amazing. I wished my momma had come with me. She would have crawled up here and I could have hung out with her vanilla smell instead of sweat and old food. She was beautiful, my momma, and almost always had a big smile on her pink lips.

After a while I was starting to get hungry, and could smell the pepperoni pizza all the way through the four corners, two ladders, and thirty-seven joints I had passed through. I was surprised that it could snake itself through all of those twists and turns, but it did, and it found me, and made my stomach rumble. More kids came through, most of them crawling over me without even stopping. A few of them talked to me, and I just shrugged in answer. No one from my school came up, though. I would know them. They were all still busy at the video games, I guess.

I looked to my left, which I was sure was my left, because your thumb and index finger make a capital L on your left hand if you hold them up, and saw the slide going to the ball pit in the distance. I crawled over eleven, ten, nine, eight, seven, six, five, four, three, two, and, finally, the last joint until I was peering down the slide into the ball bin. For a second, I panicked and turned around. There were way too many kids in that ball bin, all screaming at each other and throwing balls everywhere. My blue tunnel seemed a lot safer, especially eleven joints back. But then there were lots of kids behind me. I wasn't even sure where they had come from. Had they all been in the tunnel with me? Then they were pushing me, yelling, 'Go. Go. Go.' I clutched the sides of the blue slide and wedged my feet against the edges, hanging on for life.

One girl finally made her way right behind me and said, 'Just go, freak.'

And she pushed me as hard as she could, ripping my hands away from the sides and sending me down the slide and into the ball bin, right on top of two little boys.

They started crying, one saying that I had kicked him in the head, the other saying that I had stepped on his hand. And their mommas came up to me and said, 'Be more careful of the little kids next time,' their faces all frowning and their foreheads scrunched up like they were mad at me, when it wasn't even my fault. It reminded me of the time my momma got mad at me for pooping in my pants three years ago, and I started crying and yelling and couldn't stop for anything.

I just lay down in the ball bin and tried to bury myself underneath the balls. I didn't care if I died or not there in the ball bin. I let all of those kids jump all over me, throw balls at me, and I wailed. I wanted to be a good boy. I tried so hard to be good. My momma was counting on me and I couldn't disappoint her. And here I was, hurting little kids, making them cry, making their mommas wrinkle up their foreheads, because they were angry at me. So the tears started flowing and my nose started leaking, and I was trying to put as many balls as possible on top of me and wiggle down into them so that nobody could see me, and they would all just leave me alone. Then I felt a tug under my armpits and two big, rough hands pulled me up and away from those mean ladies and their stupid kids. The hands belonged to a tall man with brown hair and a blue baseball cap on, the same guy by the claw game. I figured he had come over to monitor the ball bin, but I still didn't see a name tag on his shirt. He wiped my nose on the bottom of his shirt, looked down at my chest, and said, 'Hey, Pepper. Do you remember me?'

I looked at him for a second. I could always remember people's faces, but it took me a minute sometimes, because I had to put together the eighty-six pictures that made up a face. I might have met him before, but if I hadn't put the pictures together then I might only remember one part of him, like his chin or his nose. I didn't seem to remember his face, but I knew that he had been standing by the claw game. I remembered his outline. The way he leaned against the column and watched the kids try to win at the claw game that never let you win. I didn't know his name, but I was so glad that he saved me from drowning in that ball bin.

'I'm your Uncle Dan.' He smiled big and I could see that he had a gold tooth at the back of his mouth, just like my momma did. But I still didn't know his face. He looked hopeful for a second, but then realized that I didn't remember him and put on what looked like a sad face to me. It was hard to tell what sadness was, but when my momma and I practiced 'feelings,' she would frown to show she was sad and smile to show she was happy.

'You really don't remember me? I'm your mom's brother, Uncle Dan. You just haven't seen me in a few years, so maybe you forgot.'

I didn't answer him. But I don't forget faces after I get the 86 pictures lined up right. And my momma's brother's name was Uncle Meanie, or at least that's what we called him.

'Come on, Pepper. Let's go to the bathroom and get you cleaned up. You're a mess, boy.'

He took me to the bathroom, and washed my hands and face, making me blow all of the snot out of my nose onto a wad of toilet paper, like my momma did when I had one of my 'fits,' as she called them. I felt better after that, the cold water was nice on my face, and my head was clearer after I got some of the snot out of it.

'No more crying, okay?' Uncle Dan pulled my name tag off and stuck it in his pocket. He was going to get in big trouble for that. Mrs. Walton had told us not to take our name tags off, no matter what. He saw my phone number on my arm then, the eights rolling along my skin, and frowned. 'Here, I have a sweatshirt for you. It's kind of cold in this place, don't you think?'

I didn't think it was that cold, but I stood there while he pulled a hoodie out of his jacket pocket. I couldn't believe he could fit an entire hoodie in that little pocket, but he did. It was gray, not my favorite color, but I slipped it on anyway and put the hood over my head, covering my ears, which is how I always wore mine to school. It was like my own private tent for my head.

'I'll get you a Dr Pepper and some ice cream, and then you'll be happy, right?'

I didn't know how he knew I loved Dr Pepper and ice cream, but they were my favorites. We walked toward the drink machine. There was a lady behind the counter, one of the blue shirt workers. Her name tag said 'Paulena.'

'Can I help you?' she asked.

'Yeah,' he answered. 'I'd like to get my nephew here a Dr Pepper and an ice cream. He can't get enough of them.'

She smiled at me and handed him a giant cup with 17 balloons on it.

'Cone or cup for the ice cream?'

'Cone,' he answered without asking me.

'What flavor?' she smiled back.

He hesitated for a second, but didn't take his eyes off her face.

'He loves chocolate, don't you?' He patted me on the shoulder, a little too hard, so I nodded. I did like chocolate, and vanilla too. But I figured today I would have chocolate.

'There you go. Enjoy your stay at That Amazing Pizza Place, where it's always an amazing day.'

He filled up the cup and turned back to her.

'Have you got a lid for this drink? We don't want him spilling it in the car.'

Paulena had a funny look on her face. 'Oh. It's to go? I didn't realize you were leaving.' She turned to me. 'Didn't you just get here with the school group a little while ago?'

He pressed his hand into my shoulder, harder this time. 'Nope. He's with me. We've been here for over two hours. It's one of our favorite places to go together.' He paused for a second and flashed a smile at Paulena. 'Anybody ever tell you how pretty your eyes are?'

The girl's face turned red.

'Really, so you model? If not, you should definitely consider it. You're a natural beauty. You must hear that all the time.'

I wasn't so sure that she was pretty, but she had Dr Pepper and ice cream, so she was all right by me.

She smiled and tucked her hair back under the baseball cap. 'Uh, no. Thanks, though.'

She reached under the counter. 'Here's your top for the drink, and a straw. Have an amazing day!'

I wasn't that ready to leave since I hadn't even ridden on the go-carts yet, but he steered me toward the swooshing doors that led outside. He held my drink for me and grabbed my hand when we got out there. He walked much faster than me, his long legs taking huge strides across the parking lot. I was having to jog a little to keep up, and tried to lick my ice cream cone at the same time. It was a lot for an eight-year-old to do. We walked across 61 of the 124 yellow lines to get to his truck. It was a nice truck, one of those kinds that you had to climb up four stairs to get into; it was green and the seats were gray. I hoped it had a great air conditioner, so my ice cream wouldn't melt all over my hands.

'Here, I'll strap you in,' he said. And, as he did, I realized that he didn't have a booster seat for me. He was just putting the seatbelt on me in a regular seat, a big boy seat. My momma told me I had to have a booster seat until I was ten. I had only turned eight on February 15, so I paused for a second and looked at Uncle Dan's blue baseball cap. It had a red 'A' on the front. I wondered what that stood for. Amazing? Still, he had the gold tooth in the back of his mouth, so I figured he was okay. I thought for a few minutes about Mrs. Walton, Jonah's momma, and Rosalind with her sticky hands. I guessed they were all still playing Skee-Ball and would probably be there when we got back since our field trip didn't end until 1:45 pm.

'You're not much of a talker, are you?' he said, as he started up the truck. It had a clock in the dashboard like my momma's car, and the numbers read 10:52 am. He had driven 108,452 miles in that truck. It said so right on the dashboard in blue lights. His hands were shaking, so I guessed he was nervous driving. Like Christopher. Driving was hard, that much I knew, too many things to count to be able to read all of the signs and watch your speed at the same time. I had watched my momma do it and she never seemed nervous, but I think she had had a lot of practice.

I shook my head 'no' to answer him. He pulled out of the parking lot and turned up the radio until it hurt my ears. I dropped my ice cream cone onto the floor and covered my ears with my hands. 'No, no, no, no, no.' I shook my head, trying to drown out the bass and tinny voice that hurt with every beat.

'Whoa,' Uncle Dan said. 'Hang on. Don't make such a mess, Pepper.' He found a towel on the floor of the truck and grabbed the ice cream cone. 'You want me to turn it down?'

I nodded, but kept my hands over my ears until he turned the music down really low. My ice cream cone was covered in grass and dirt from the floor, but I didn't care. I was done with it anyway. He didn't seem mad at me at all for spilling the ice cream on the floor. He tried to give me the ice cream again, and when I shook my head he put it on the towel on the floor.

'We'll get you a new ice cream cone soon. Okay?'

I didn't ask him where we were going, but I thought I might be in trouble. You were never supposed to go anywhere without telling Mrs. Walton, and I had forgotten all about that when we were getting the ice cream and Dr Pepper. She was definitely going to put me into time out and maybe even write a note home to my momma. I hated it when she sent notes home. My momma would try to get the story out of me, and, even though I really wanted to tell her my side of it, most of the time I couldn't get the words out. 'I don't know,' I'd end up saying, after I had tried telling her over and over and the words got stuck between my brain and my mouth. Then she would have to go and talk to my teacher, who never knew my side of the story either. I wanted to make her proud of me, so I did my best to try to act good, but I knew I was going to be in big trouble today. I bit my fingernails and worried about what she would say.

I started counting the white lines as he drove out onto the interstate, until I was at 1,792, and we got to the old bridge that crossed the Mississippi River. I knew where we were, because if you looked at the new bridge you could see it was an M, like McDonald's, my favorite place to eat. My momma had taught me the letter M by showing me that bridge. Counting lines helped me to calm down. And I started to forget how mad Mrs. Walton was going to be about me leaving without telling her.

His hands had quit shaking by then, so I guess he was calmer too. He started to talk to me. 'The thing is,' he said, 'I loved your momma so much. She was my favorite sister.'

I wondered how many sisters he had. I only knew one of her brothers, Uncle Meanie, until Uncle Dan showed up.

'When we were kids, we had the best time playing down at the lake. I would scare her with lizards and frogs. She was such a great baby sister.'

I thought about my brother and sister, Christopher and Sabrina. They were the best brother and sister ever, even if Sabrina sometimes acted very bad and yelled at my momma. 'She's a teenager,' Momma said, as if that explained the yelling. I just covered my ears and hoped that she would stop. But once every thirty-seven days, as if on a schedule, she would start yelling and my momma would yell back, and then, before you knew it, somebody was crying and they put me to bed.

'It will all be better in the morning,' my momma would say. 'Everybody feels better in the morning. You don't worry your head about this, Pepper. You just snuggle up and have good dreams.'

I believed her. My momma always told the truth. And she was right; things were better in the morning and Sabrina was nice again.

Uncle Dan started to cry. His face scrunched up and big tears rolled down his cheeks. I wasn't sure what to do. I had never seen a grown man cry before.

'That's why it pains me, pains me, I tell you, to give you the bad news.'

I sat up straight. It was like a bolt of lightning went through me. I didn't like bad news. I didn't like grown men crying. I wanted to be back at That Amazing Pizza Place with Rosalind Jane, Mrs. Walton, and Jonah's momma. I didn't like this at all. And I wasn't sure that Uncle Dan was my uncle.

'There was an accident. And your mom has gone to heaven. They called me to come and get you.'

I looked at his face again, only the side of it this time. He had whiskers that were growing in, some gray, some brown, and, for a second, I thought about trying to count them all. Maybe then he would stop talking, stop telling me about my momma. I couldn't hear this, couldn't understand anything else he said after saying that my momma had died. I couldn't stand being in this car with this man who I didn't even know. He didn't know the game. He didn't know how to survive. We would never make it out if Momma wasn't there. I took a deep breath and screamed, 'MAMMMMMAAAA' as loud as I could, making it last until I ran out of breath. Then I did it again, 'MAMMMMMAAAAA!'

I watched the clock on the dashboard and his hands on the steering wheel. The minutes changed from seven to eight, to nine, then ten, eleven, and twelve. His hands kept gripping the steering wheel tighter and tighter with each passing minute. But I kept screaming. I missed my momma and I wanted her back, accident or no accident. No other words came out of my mouth. Most of the time it worked. If you yelled the one thing you wanted loud enough, over and over, somebody would try really hard to get you what you asked for. And, right then, I wanted my momma back more than anything in the whole world. Even if she grounded me. Even if I could never play Xbox or watch *SpongeBob SquarePants* again, I wanted my momma.

I took a deep breath. 'MAMMMMAAAAAAA!'

I caught a quick glimpse of his fist before the world went black.

Chapter 2

I woke up to 387 lines across the ceiling of a room I'd never been in before. It was beaded board, I knew. We had had it on the porch of my house, and in the bathroom, and in my brother's room. My momma loved beaded board, and I loved getting lost in the lines of it, their interlocking sides, and the way they ran across the ceiling from end to end. I liked counting the seams where they met, butting up against each other like they were holding up the world. So I was happy to see those lines again, but I had no idea where I was.

My head hurt when I moved it. I could lie there still, and it was okay, but the minute I tried to sit up, or even turn to one side or the other, it felt like a hammer was pounding into my brain and the room started spinning. I put my hand up to the side of my head, and could feel a bump there, about the size of my fist, pulsing with my heartbeat. I counted seventy-two beats of my heart in that bump before I turned back to the ceiling. I had never felt my heart in my head before. I wondered if it had moved from my chest to the inside of my head. I hoped that, if it had, it wouldn't make me forget my mom or my brother and sister. Tears started to sting the corners of my eyes, so I started recounting the lines on the boards across the ceiling to try to make them go away. She couldn't be in heaven. I just knew it.

The door opened and I heard the floor creak with the seven steps that came toward the bed.

'Hey there, Pepper. How you doing?'

I heard Uncle Dan's voice, but didn't move my head or my eyes to look at him.

'Here, I brought you an ice pack. You sure have a big bump there.'

He came into my view, standing over my face with a blue bag in his hand. He still had on the baseball cap with the red 'A.' He put the cold pack against my bump, and I winced at the pain.

'This will help, I promise. You have to be more careful, boy. You really hit your head when I had to stop real fast so I didn't hit the car in front of us. You can't just go unbuckling your seatbelt like that.' He paused. 'You're liable to get yourself thrown out the window. Or even worse.'

I squinted into his eyes, which I didn't like doing, but it helped if I made my eyes narrow. He looked away toward the corner of the room, so I knew he was lying. Plus I remembered his hand coming toward my face. I never could get why people lied when telling the truth was so much easier. Heck, just getting the words to come out right was hard enough. I could never understand lying. You had to say the opposite of what you meant and then pretend like that was what you meant in the first place.

'Good thing I blocked you from hitting the windshield. Otherwise you might have ended up in the hospital.' He pressed the ice pack gently onto my bump.

I was confused. I was pretty sure he was lying. I wasn't sure that Uncle Dan had saved me. I was almost positive that I saw his hand coming toward my face, closed fist. I wasn't even sure he was my Uncle Dan. I couldn't remember seeing him before I did at the claw game at That Amazing Pizza Place, not in a picture or anything. And my momma never talked about my Uncle Dan, only Uncle Meanie, who was always really nice to me. I wasn't even sure why we called him Uncle Meanie, but I remembered what he looked like, and he was not this guy. And then I thought about my momma and remembered what he had told me in the car. I opened my mouth to yell again, and he clamped his hand over it. His hand smelled like dirt, which was making me gag, so I closed my mouth and tried not to breathe it in.

'Now, you're a big boy. Enough of that yelling.' He paused for a second to see if I was going to scream again. 'I know it's hard. It's hard on all of us. But I loved your momma and I promised her I would take good care of you. You have to let me do that. It's what she wanted.'

I focused on his whiskers and tried to breathe through my nose, which was kind of stopped up, but I couldn't breathe any other way without feeling like I was going to throw up. Focusing on his whiskers was easier than trying to take in his whole face. I didn't believe him, though. I was pretty sure he was a liar, which I only said in my head because, well, he had his hand over my mouth, but also because my mom told me never to call people that. I could feel the truth in the bottom of my stomach, though, lying there, waiting for the right time to come up to my mouth.

'A promise is a promise. Can you help me keep this one to your momma?'

I nodded and started counting his whiskers. I had heard once that the average man has between 7,000 and 15,000 whiskers. I was sure that Uncle Dan leaned toward the 15,000 end of the range. And I was pretty sure that he was lying about my momma dying. That just could not be true. I knew her. I loved her. I could still feel her. I was sure that my stomach would feel empty if she were really, truly dead.

He took his hand off my mouth finally, and said, 'Now remember. I'm here to take care of you now. That's what your momma wanted. Don't you want to make her happy?'

I wondered if dead people could be happy. If you don't have a body, do you have feelings? She wasn't dead though, so she probably did have feelings. And

I always wanted to make her happy. I just knew she was alive. It should be easy to know the truth. You shouldn't have to rely on how your stomach feels. I knew one thing that made my momma really happy though: the fact that I could always remember her seven numbers: 373-1888.

'Here, hold this on your head,' he said. 'But don't press too hard. Twenty minutes on, twenty minutes off. I'll be right back.'

I didn't have a watch, so I started counting the seconds as he walked out of the room. I lifted off the ice pack, smelled it, licked it, and then pressed my palm quietly onto the egg that seemed implanted into my forehead. It hurt, but I wanted to see how bad it was. I bet it was blue, maybe even the color of an Easter egg. I was gentle, but it hurt, one of those kinds of hurts that feels good when you press on it, like digging around in your foot for a splinter.

I heard the toilet flush and he walked back into the room. I tried to make my eyes focus on Uncle Dan's face. I knew I needed to remember what he looked like. I needed to know who was taking care of me. If I got lost again, I knew I would need to find him. Just for a little while, until I got my mom's numbers dialed. Then I needed to make sure I could point him out when the time came, and I knew the time would come. Either way, I memorized every single line and mark on his face. I counted his wrinkles, six at the corner of each eye, four that cut into his forehead, two that ran beside the corners of his mouth. His eyes were blue and it looked like he had lost half of one eyebrow. His teeth were white and straight, like my mom's, and that gold one showed up in the back when he smiled.

He helped me get out of bed. I was dizzy and, even though I was about to pee in my pants, I was scared to run from him. I started kind of dancing a little, trying not to have an accident. He led me by the arm into the bathroom. At least he understood the peepee dance without me having to tell him.

'Now just take it easy. We have to give you time to get your head back on straight after that bump. It might take a week or so.'

I just nodded. I figured out that I could be quiet around Uncle Dan and he wouldn't mind, not like Momma, who had always made me talk to her. I peed and he made me wash my hands. I glanced down at his. They were clean, mostly, but his fingernails had dirt under them and one of his nails looked like an aquarium holding in blood. Maybe he had hit it with a hammer or something. He led me into the kitchen and sat me down at the table. It was a picnic table, right in the middle of the kitchen.

I looked around his kitchen. It was smaller than my momma's and not nearly as clean. But Momma said that men were dirtier than women, and not as good cooks, even though she was teaching me how to cook so that I could be a fry cook when I got older. That's what SpongeBob was, and I figured I could be one too.

He walked toward the stove and turned on the gas with a whoosh. Blue flames lit up under the skillet and he cracked four eggs into a bowl, added some milk, and then stirred them up with a fork really fast. He added salt and pepper before putting them into the pan with a sizzle. I hated eggs. They smelled like poop and they felt like wet snails in my mouth.

He put the scrambled eggs and toast on the table along with a glass of milk for me. It wasn't chocolate. I sniffed the food and retched, leaning over the side of the table, gagging. The movement made my head swim, while my eyes tried to catch up with my brain.

'No, no, no, no, no,' I said, quietly though, so he wouldn't clamp his hand over my mouth again. 'No.' I shook my head, listening to my brain rattle in there. I wasn't going to be able to eat those eggs. Eggs made me gag. They're not white. They're yellow and runny, and I just knew that if I put one in my mouth it would drip down the back of my throat, and I would throw it all up, which always made my momma so mad. Tears came to my eyes, and I looked up at Uncle Dan with another 'No.'

'What's wrong?' he asked. 'They're from my chickens out back.'

I walked carefully over to the window, one sock foot in front of the other, keeping my head level so that I wouldn't fall down. I loved chickens. My mom had a friend who had six chickens and one rooster. She would let me feed them when I went to her house. Chickens were my favorite besides puppy dogs. Chickens never jumped up on you and you could pet the nice ones. I liked the way their feathers folded on top of each other, making them smooth when you petted them the right way. Plus, chickens pretty much only said one word: 'Cheeeek' is what it sounded like, but I knew that 'cheeeek' from a chicken could mean, 'I'm starving to death over here,' 'There's a dog trying to kill me,' or even, 'Hey, I laid an egg.' It was all in how they said it. I thought that should be the way people should talk, with only one word that meant everything instead of words that floated around in your head, just out of reach when you needed them.

'Not there. That's the front yard.'

I looked out and only saw a field with a dirt driveway that disappeared up the hill.

'There.' He pointed across the room. 'The back yard is that way.'

I put one sock foot in front of the other again and walked 23 steps to the other side of the room. I kept my head at the same level and my eyes looking straight forward. The minute they looked to the side, the room started spinning again. I found the window and saw seven chickens running around the coop, two white, one black, and four speckled. I wondered if they could get out of there, if I could pet them.

'And that guy is the rooster, Brutus, because he's a brute.' Uncle Dan came up beside me and pointed to a big black bird over in the corner. 'He's kind of mean, so steer clear of him. He tends to peck people on the calf when they're not looking. The hens are nice, though.'

He stopped for a minute and put his hand on top of my head. I flinched, but made myself not pull away from him.

'I don't name the hens, 'cause, well, they're just hens. And eventually you're going to have to eat them for dinner, so why name 'em, you know?'

I didn't answer, so he asked, 'You like chickens?'

I nodded, put my hand up to my forehead to feel my egg. It still hurt. I wondered if my head was going to hatch an egg like the chickens did. He frowned at me, which I knew meant that he was sad or mad or, even worse, disappointed, so I took my hand away.

'Good, then. That can be your chore, feeding the chickens and staying out of Brutus' way. I'll show you how to do it after breakfast. You can even gather the eggs. It's like hide and seek. Sometimes you have to search for them. Now come on back over here to the table and eat some of this good food I made for you before it gets cold.' He handed me the ice pack and we went toward the table.

I walked to the table, but promised myself that there was no way I was ever going to eat an egg. I looked at them and tried to figure out how mad Uncle Dan would be if I didn't eat them. I only liked them at Easter. I liked the way you could layer the colors on top of each other until it made brown, but I didn't even eat the ones I dyed. I gagged again when I saw the eggs and looked over at the toast.

I saw his smile turn upside down again out of the corner of my eye, but his hands stayed wrapped around his cup of coffee, so I thought I was pretty safe.

I picked up a piece of toast, and sniffed it. Uncle Dan had smeared butter on it. Gag again. There was no way I could eat that. I knew Uncle Dan was going to get mad at me for that.

I started to cry, very quietly, but let the tears roll down, wetting the hoodie that he had given me yesterday.

He looked at me and seemed confused. 'Boy, what the heck am I supposed to feed you?'

I didn't answer, but just put my head down on the table, on my good side, the one without the egg on it, and watched my tears fall onto my jeans. My head started spinning again, feeling like my eyes were going in circles in their sockets.

He got up and walked eight steps back toward the stove. I heard him open the refrigerator, then the pan sizzle.

'Hang on, Pepper. Quit crying already. You're way too big for all of that crying stuff.'

I wiped away my tears and walked back over to the window to look out at the chickens. There was something about them that I had always liked. Maybe it was the way they felt so soft, but had those sharp claws and beaks. They could take care of themselves when they needed to. I had read about them in science. They could pick all kinds of bugs and stuff out of the ground, and if you didn't put them in a cage, then they pretty much took care of themselves. They really liked eating ticks, which was fine by me, because ticks sucked your blood and creeped me out. Like little vampires that you don't see until they are filled up with your blood. I had gotten one under my arm once. Momma heated up some tweezers with a match, then pulled it off me, saying, 'You have to be really careful or you'll leave the head in there. And then it will just grow its body back.' I screamed while she did it, but tried to be still and brave for her.

Plus, chickens can fly if they really need to get away from something. I wished that I could fly. Then I would be able to see how to fly home and find my momma. The only bad thing for chickens was coyotes and some dogs. They didn't get along with chickens at all. I didn't know if there were coyotes here, but I reminded myself to ask Uncle Dan after breakfast.

I decided I would feed them, and not just because Uncle Dan told me that was my 'chore.' I knew about chores. My mom used to make me put up the toilet paper, but we only had one drawer to put it in. So I would make a big pyramid on the back of the toilet. If you lined up the rolls just right, they wouldn't topple over when you sat down. But you had to get the spacing perfect. I was good at it.

I wanted to feed those chickens so I could get to know them. Then I would pick out names for each one of them. Everybody deserved to have a special name, even if you did have to eat them in the end. I stood there for a while, watching them peck at the ground and each other. I even laughed a little, because chickens are funny if you watch the way they walk with their chests all puffed out, and they don't even fall down.

'Okay, what about this?' Uncle Dan came back to the table and brought some bacon, laid out onto a paper towel, which soaked up the grease.

I leaned over and sniffed, then smiled. Bacon, I loved bacon. I could eat bacon all day. Bacon smelled like somebody was grilling salt. It was the best thing I'd smelled all day. And I liked the way it crunched in your mouth when you bit into it. But there was one big problem: he only had six pieces.

I picked one up, sniffed it again, licked it, and stuffed it into my mouth. I was starving. I hadn't eaten since yesterday, and that was only a little bit of ice cream for lunch.

That made Uncle Dan's face crack into a smile. 'Oh, so you like bacon, huh? Well, I like bacon too.'

He shoved a piece in his mouth and I frowned, pulling the plate closer to me so that I could eat all of it. I mean, he had eggs and all of that buttered toast. Surely he would give me the bacon.

He laughed. 'Okay then, Pepper. You eat the bacon. I'll eat the eggs and toast.' He paused. 'Toast is good. You should try toast some time. We gotta get some meat on your bones, boy.'

I wasn't sure what he was talking about since I was eating meat at the time. He pinched my side to show me I was skinny.

He pushed the milk toward me, which I just sniffed at, and then he finally gave me a cup of water. I wanted the chai tea that my momma always made me. The sweet cinnamon taste calmed me down when things got too swirly for me. I was pretty sure that Uncle Dan had never even heard of chai tea, and that we would probably have a hard time finding any out here in the country. We needed a grocery store, a Kroger, the kind they had in Memphis, Tennessee, where I used to live. Where my momma still did, I was sure.

I wanted to tell him that, besides bacon, I really only liked white food, and Happy Meals from McDonald's, only not the apples, and pepperoni pizza. I wanted him to buy me some Dr Pepper, in the little cans, and keep them in the fridge so that I could get one in the afternoons after school, like at home. I wasn't even sure if I was going to go to school anymore. And, if I did, would it be my old school? Would we drive that far every day? If we did, I just knew my momma would come and pick me up like she always did. If she were alive. I went back and forth on it. I wasn't always sure.

I wanted to ask him about the coyotes. But it was easier just to listen to the pounding of my heart in the egg on my head, keep quiet, and eat the bacon. There were too many words in the world, and people talked way too much. I was trying to even things out by not filling up the air with more words than it could hold at one time.

After breakfast, Uncle Dan showed me around his house. He told me, 'This is the greatest place you'll ever live.'

I wasn't so sure about that. I liked my house better, mostly because my momma was there, but also because it was cleaner, and nicer, and had lots and lots of Legos. Uncle Dan had the usual rooms, a den, a kitchen and dining room combination, a long hallway with two bedrooms at the end, one for me and one for him. It was kind of a plain house, with cinderblock walls. I thought only prisons were made out of cinderblock, but I didn't ask Uncle Dan that.

Uncle Dan had a satellite dish in the back yard that he showed me. That was the best part about his house. He told me that he could get 496 channels, which was the coolest thing I had ever heard. He told me to pick a channel, any channel. My momma didn't even have cable at all, only Netflix streaming, which was great to watch *Phineas and Ferb*, but I had seen all of those episodes over and over. I wasn't sure what channel to ask him to put on. Channel A5? Or 4,356? I had only seen tv in hotels and just used the up and down button on the remote control. So I kept my mouth shut. I had learned that if I let other people do the talking they would usually fig-ure it out for me.

But he just stood there in the den, in front of the biggest tv I had ever seen, and waited. 'So, what's it going to be, boy? What channel do you want to watch?'

I took a guess. 'How about channel 48?' Forty-eight was a great number, but I had no idea if it had cartoons on it.

'Forty-eight? What's on channel 48? Is that the Food Network?'

I just shrugged and we waited for the channel to pop up. It was CNN.

'You gotta tell me what you want to watch. There's a whole slew of shows, and they're on 24-7.'

I shrugged.

'Me? I like football and NASCAR. We'll watch some football on Saturday.'

I didn't know what 24-7 was, but I thought maybe that was a channel with cartoons or something.

'Come on, Pepper. Help me out here.'

I thought I could watch *Phineas and Ferb* over again. I had seen all of them like a million times, but they were funny. 'Can you get *Phineas and Ferb*?'

'What's *Phineas and Ferb*?' He looked at me kind of strange, like he had never heard of it.

I thought about how to answer him. 'You know.' I sang the theme song.

I wasn't sure if he wanted me to go on, but he just stood there holding the remote, so I did. Then I stopped. Even though it was right in the middle of the song. I thought maybe he would chime in and finish the song with me. But he didn't.

Uncle Dan beamed, his whiskers widening over his big smile. I could even see his gold tooth, just like Momma's, when he smiled that big. 'He speaks! I knew I could get you to speak! You even sing! Hey, man, you're a pretty good singer. I like the fast part at the end.'

He took off his hat and ran his hand through his hair. 'I've never heard of *Phineas and Ferb*, but I like the song. I get twenty-nine channels for kids. You think it's on one of them?'

I nodded and shifted my weight between my feet so that one of them didn't get too tired.

'Now those I can find. Sometimes I like to watch them myself. Reminds me of being a kid, well, and having my own boy.' His breath caught for a minute, somewhere deep inside of his chest, maybe near his heart. Then he swallowed hard and said, 'Here. I'll show you.'

He showed me the remote, well, all three remotes, which seemed impossible to use. I was pretty good at electronics, but I wasn't sure I could ever get the hang of all of those remotes.

'You just push this main power button on, which turns on the tv, the satellite, and the remote access box, and, then, you're in business. You can watch any of the twenty-nine cartoon channels you want.'

I smiled at him, trying to show him that I was happy. I knew that I should use a smile when I was happy, and twenty-nine channels of all cartoons made me really happy.

'I'll leave you to watch the cartoons. I'll stick to the sports, plus some CMT every now and then.' He flipped over to some guys playing football and sat down on the couch. It was light blue and nubby. I could tell even though I hadn't felt it yet. I wondered if it would imprint on the back of my legs when I did.

'Oh yeah,' he said. 'Go, man, run!'

I just sort of stood there and counted the pulses in the egg on my forehead. It was like he had completely forgotten that we were looking for cartoons. I watched him staring at the game. The guys on the tv had a football, that much I knew, but I didn't know the rules of the game.

'Score!' he yelled, jumping to his feet as the guy on the tv ran to the end of the field with the ball tucked under his arm like a baby.

I looked up at Uncle Dan. He was taller than I thought, and he was kind of in a daze, yelling at the tv, dancing around the den, but then he remembered me standing there and woke up. 'Here, you want a try?'

I took the black remote in both hands.

'Do. Not. Drop. It.'

He made me nervous. I didn't really understand. I dropped our Wii remote all of the time and it never broke. How breakable was a remote anyway?

I tried the up and down on the channel, finding *SpongeBob SquarePants* on the Cartoon Network pretty fast. I turned up the volume with the gray remote and handed them both back to Uncle Dan, a smile plastered on my face. I had no idea what to do with the second black remote.

I watched SpongeBob trying to learn to drive. I had seen this one 32 times, and remembered every line by heart.

'Now you got the hang of it,' he said, and raised his hand in the air.

It took me a second. I wasn't sure what he was doing, but I looked away from the tv just in time to see his hand go up. I flinched and jumped back a step, getting dizzy with the sudden movement. For a second, I thought he might hit me. Or that I might fall down. Or that he might hit me and I would fall down. I wasn't sure my head could take another hit.

His face fell. He was so happy just a second before, but then his face just dropped like it was going to fall onto the ground and he frowned at me.

'Pepper,' he said. 'It's okay. I'm not going to hurt you.' He stopped talking and knelt down in front of me to look at me in the eyes. I tried looking to the ground, but he got his eyes in the way again.

'I would never do that.' His look was hard, right into both of my eyes, like he could read my mind. It felt like déjà vu. My mom had explained it to me, seeing again. Remembering a dream in real life. I wasn't sure I had ever had one, but I liked the way the words rolled through my head. I closed my eyes so I wouldn't have to look at him for long. Faces were hard enough. Eyes were really hard. They moved faster than my brain did.

'Fist bump for getting the hang of the remotes so fast. Great job!'

I smiled and held my fist in the air, our knuckles touching for a moment when they bumped together. His skin was dark against mine, his hand rough and calloused. I tried to remember back to the car before everything went black. I was pretty sure he had hit me on the head with that same fist. Either way, I was going to be careful around him and not give him anymore reasons to hit me.

Again, Uncle Dan, the mind reader, said, 'Don't worry so much, boy. I'd never hit you. I'm going to take care of you now.'

He turned back to the tv and flipped the channel away from *SpongeBob SquarePants*. 'Now, let's watch some football!'

Chapter 3

On Sunday morning Uncle Dan woke me up early to go fishing. My head heard his 18 steps down the hall and the seven across the room, but my eyes were still sleeping. They were tired and didn't want to wake up. I felt his hand on my shoulder, shaking me a little, and heard him saying, 'Pepper, it's time to get up. We're going to have the best time today.'

I cracked one eye. It was mostly still dark outside, and I had no idea why anyone would want to get up that early in the morning. I had never been fishing before and didn't think I would like it. I rolled over and the room spun again. I made my head be still and pulled my blanket over it. It was kind of scratchy, but muffled Uncle Dan's voice a little bit. If I closed my eyes, the spinning mostly stopped.

'Come on. The fish are all out there waiting on us. You won't believe what big fish there are, right there swimming in our lake.'

'Grrrr,' I growled at him, hoping he'd go away and leave me alone.

He surprised me by yanking the covers off the bed. I rolled up into a ball, tucking my head under my arms, just in case. I watched the dresser spin sideways before my eyes caught up with my brain again. I closed them to make it stop.

'Pepper. Cut that out. Seriously. We're going fishing and you're going to love it.'

I cracked an eye open again. He was dressed in shorts and a t-shirt that said, 'Bass Pro Shop.' I knew because I could read just about anything that I wanted to read. 'I'll stay here and watch *SpongeBob* until you get back,' I told him. I knew how to work the remote; I could stay by myself.

'You can't stay by yourself, Pepper. You're six. No six-year-olds get to stay by themselves.'

I shook my head no again.

'What?' he asked.

'Not six. Eight.'

'You're not eight. Obviously you're not eight.'

'Eight,' I said. I knew how old I was.

'You're only in second grade. And you're too little to be eight.'

'Eight,' I said. 'I know how old I am.'

'Okay,' he sighed. 'Get up and eat some bacon if you're eight years old.'

I crawled out of bed, feeling the cool wood beneath my feet and counting the steps down the hall and into the kitchen.

We sat down at the table. It had a pattern on it that spun in circles, or maybe that was my egg making my head spin again. I liked the metal that went around the edges of the table. It gave me something to hold onto to steady myself.

He had a big plate of bacon and some toast, without butter, on the table.

'Try the toast,' he said.

I picked up a piece. I smelled it. It smelled okay, like burnt crumbs. I put it against my cheek and it felt scratchy against my skin.

Uncle Dan looked at me funny, like he had never felt toast against his cheek before. 'Here.' He pushed some butter over to me. 'You can put your own butter on it.'

I shook my head and touched my tongue to the toast.

'No butter?'

I shook my head again and took the smallest bite I could. I crunched it between my front teeth to check out the texture.

'You are one funny kid, Pepper.'

I took another bite. Toast wasn't so bad. Bacon was better, but toast with no butter was pretty good, too. It scratched the roof of my mouth a little, but in a good way.

Still, I didn't want to go fishing. 'I'm eight. I can stay by myself.'

'No eight-year-old can stay alone, Pepper. You have to be twelve to stay by yourself.' He stopped talking and looked hard at my face. 'I remember the day you were born,' he said. 'Your mom was so proud. She was lying up there in the hospital bed, and you were right in her arms, all bundled up in this blue blanket. And you weren't even crying. You were a really good baby.'

I squinted my eyes when he mentioned my momma. The bit of toast sat in my mouth while I stopped chewing. His lies made me want to throw up. I had seen the pictures. My blanket wasn't blue. It was white with blue and pink stripes, the kind that they give every baby in the hospital. My momma had told me that they give every baby a blanket and a matching hat when they are born. Plus, if he was there the day I was born, then how come he didn't know that I was eight instead of six.

I finished my toast and walked back toward the bedroom where I slept. I got into the bed and put my head under the covers where it was quiet and nobody was trying to tell me things that I knew were not true. My brain didn't work like other people's but I was no dummy, that's for sure. I knew my momma wouldn't lie to me and neither would pictures. I remembered the pictures of my momma holding me and that blanket was not blue.

'Come on, Pepper,' he called down the hall.

I heard him walking around, clanging stuff together, putting ice into his cooler. I wondered if he was mad again. I counted numbers in my head, since I couldn't find anything to count under the covers, except for the freckles on my arms, and it was too dark to see them anyway. When I got to

1,408, Uncle Dan walked into the room. He didn't pull back the covers, but talked like he didn't know where I was.

'Man, I'm so tired. I was going to go fishing, but now I'm just feeling like I need to take a nap.' He stopped and walked around the room for a few seconds, eleven steps, then he yawned really loudly.

'I just didn't get any sleep last night. Maybe I'll just take a quick nap for a little while.'

He walked toward the bed, four steps.

'This bed looks so comfy. So fluffy with all of the covers on it.'

I could feel him standing next to the bed. He yawned again.

'I'm just going to lie down right here!' Then he jumped on top of me, squishing me into a pancake. 'Man, this bed is lumpy.'

Then he tickled me until I was laughing so hard I was about to pee. He acted like he didn't even see me until he pulled off the covers.

'Pepper! I didn't even know you were there, boy! I wondered why this bed was so lumpy.'

I smiled at him. He made me laugh. But I was going to watch him closely to see when he lied again.

'Eight,' I said, even though I was afraid I was going to make him mad.

He smiled back at me. 'Oh yeah, Mr. Eight-Year-Old? When's your birthday, smarty pants?'

I knew that answer. It was numbers. Of course I knew the day I was born. 'February 15, 2005.'

2 + 15 = 17. 2 + 15 + 2005 = 2022. And if you added up the first three numbers, two, one, and five, they made eight. Eight, that was how old I was.

'Good job. You remembered your birthday. I remember it like it was yesterday.' He looked away. 'Then eight you are,' Uncle Dan slowly moved his hand to pat me on the shoulder. 'Will you please go fishing with me?'

I thought about it. I would have to growl at him if he lied to me again. He was being really nice to me at the moment, and now he seemed to believe that I was eight. I nodded okay.

'Man,' he said. 'We're gonna have a blast. I'm gonna show you everything, how to put a cricket on the hook, how to cast the line, how to reel in the fish. I know you're going to catch something real quick, since you're so quiet. Being quiet helps, because you just sit there and wait for that fish to nibble at your bait, and then, bam, you hook it and reel it in quick.' His words rolled out of his mouth fast, like he was one of those auctioneer guys I'd seen on tv. 'I'll even clean it for you.'

I just nodded and waited for him to finish.

'Man, I love fishing. You're going to love it too.' He got up to walk out of the room. 'Of course you will. Fishing runs in our blood.'

He brought me some clothes to wear, a green t-shirt and some khaki shorts. Then he gave me some shoes that he called 'water shoes.' I hoped that I wouldn't be walking on any water while we were fishing. I wondered how he knew my shoe size before I got here. Maybe my momma told him.

'Get your clothes on, Pepper. We've got some fishing to do.'

As it turns out, I liked fishing a lot, well, after we got the hooks into the water. The best part about fishing was getting to ride in Uncle Dan's boat out on the lake. It was a little boat, green with only three seats in it, but he let me drive it once we got out into the middle of the lake. I was pretty good at it, even though he kept one hand on the stick. I turned it in a circle, then made it go in a straight line. It was kind of like playing one of Christopher's video games. I missed Christopher and his Xbox, especially playing Halo, which he let me play if my momma wasn't around every now and then.

But fishing was another matter. I liked worms, but not crickets, and I definitely didn't want to stick a hook through either of their guts. I mean, who kills a perfectly good insect by gutting them with a hook?

'Here's how you do it,' Uncle Dan said. 'You just reach down in the bucket here and pull out a cricket.'

I cringed. Those crickets had six legs. There were about 100 of them in that bucket. That's 600 legs, all wiggling around, trying to get out. And then there was the sound they made rubbing their legs together. I couldn't stand the thought of holding them in my hand, no glove or anything.

'Then you take the hook and go through his head. That way his legs will keep wiggling when you put him in the water and the fish will think he's alive.' The cricket crunched when he put the hook in. It made my skin crawl.

'And then,' he said, picking up his pole, 'you cast out your line into the water, and you watch and wait.' He handed me the pole. 'You're pretty good at watching and waiting, aren't you, Pepper?'

I nodded. That's what I always did, watched and waited, especially at school. Otherwise, I wasn't sure how to act.

People at school liked me. My momma said they treated me like I was the school mascot. I always thought a mascot was a tiger or a bear or something football teams had, so I never really understood what she was talking about. But the kids and the teachers at my school were all pretty nice to me, except that Rosalind Jane girl, who wanted to hug me all the time and tell me that we were going to get married. I didn't like her at all, and I let her know it on the first day of first grade.

I hadn't wanted to go to school anyway. I loved summer. Summer was fun. You got to sleep late, read books, play video games, go to swimming les-sons, and stay up and watch movies until 10:30 pm.

Summer rocked. School didn't rock so much. So, on that first day back, the first day of first grade, I was crying, and my momma was trying to calm me down so she could take a picture of me, but I just wanted to go back and crawl under my covers until about ten o'clock in the morning.

'Come on, Pepper. It's the first day of school. It's going to be fun.'

I was standing on the front porch of our house, our gray house, on the edge of the stairs, in my new uniform: khaki shorts, a white shirt with a collar, tucked in, and a belt. I hated the belt. It felt like someone was squeezing in my tummy, even when it was loose. Plus, I was afraid that I wouldn't be able to get it undone quick enough to make it to the bathroom. There were lots of things to worry about at school, and my belt was a new one this year. But I had on my summer sandals, which helped me to run really fast. I didn't mind the uniform, minus the belt. It was sitting in the classroom that made me cry. All of the work that I couldn't understand. I hated writing the words so much. It was hard work and the letters got all mixed up when I tried to write them down. Tears kept leaking out of my eyes. I just knew it was going to be so boring.

'You'll get to see all of your friends. Lyndon will be there. And Diego. And Dominic.'

She smiled, and I knew I was supposed to smile back at her, but I couldn't make the tears stop rolling. She had on yoga pants and a white tank top. She liked to wear yoga pants, the kind with the flower stitched onto the back of them. She said it was a lotus flower, for good luck. She loved yoga and soccer, so it was either yoga pants and her Chacos or soccer shorts and her black and white striped Sambas. I had read 'Samba' on the side of her shoe, so I knew they were the good ones. I liked the way I could tell exactly what she was going to be doing each day by what she wore. Today was yoga.

'Please, baby. Stop crying so I can take your picture. You look so handsome with your new haircut and backpack.'

I thought about my backpack. It was a Plants vs. Zombies backpack with a matching lunch box that hooked onto the outside with these cool clips. I loved my backpack. And my lunch box. They were really the only good things about school.

'I don't like school,' I told her.

She frowned for a second, and her forehead wrinkled. 'I know, love, but this year's going to be different. Plus, I packed you five carrots, a packet of Goldfish, a cheese stick, a Jolly Rancher, and saltines for lunch. And a big thermos of chai tea. All your favorites.'

'No bacon?'

She frowned again. 'Honey, we've been through this. Bacon isn't a good school food. It would be cold by the time you ate lunch.'

I didn't like food that was cold when it was supposed to be hot. She was so smart. She knew all of the tricks. 'My brain doesn't work at school. It's too hard.'

'Not this year.' She stopped and sighed. 'Didn't anyone ever tell you that second grade is a repeat of first grade? You just review everything you did last year.'

I shook my head no.

'You know, like, you did it all last year?' She leaned in close and I could smell her vanilla. She always wore vanilla, and always smelled like cookies. Then she whispered, 'Now, take a deep breath, put on a happy face, and let me take your picture, okay?'

'Let me wipe away my tears.' I wiped my eyes on her hair. She wore it long, so it was easy enough, and it made her laugh every time I did that.

'Okay, Pepper, now give me a smile.' She held up her cell phone while I tried to smile. I knew my face would be all splotchy and red from crying, but I knew she wouldn't give up until I smiled for her for first-day pictures. I looked at her face, half hidden by her cell phone. A big smile on her face, her white teeth shining in the sunlight. I liked to make her happy.

'I love you, Pepper.'

'I love you too, Momma.'

'You do?' she asked. 'How much?'

She always did that, asked me how much I loved her. I wasn't sure how to measure love. Was it in cups, inches, pounds? I didn't think that numbers could be put on how I felt about my mom. I knew that she made my heart feel big and my face smile. And I knew her answer to that question was always the same: 'More than the stars will allow.' But I was never one for copying anybody, so I made up something different each time she asked me.

'Thirty-six times.' I looked at her, hopeful that it was a good response.

'Thirty-six times is a lot,' she smiled. She lifted up her cell phone again to take another picture. I remembered the way her fingers stood out from the sides, so they wouldn't get in the way. 'Show me thirty-six times in that smile, boy.'

Click. Her phone made a click when she took the picture.

'Pepper, boy. Why are you spacing out? You have a bite, something's on the end of your line!'

I guess I was dreaming for a minute, thinking about my mom. I missed her. A lot. And I was pretty sure that she wasn't dead. She was probably looking for me, every single day. I felt a jerk in my hands, and I grabbed my fishing pole tight, while what felt like a whale pulled on the end of it. I'm not dumb. I know whales don't live in lakes, but it was big, whatever it was. I was a little scared it might pull me in, it was tugging so hard.

'Somebody help!' I looked at Uncle Dan. My stomach felt funny and I could feel sweat rolling down my back. 'Can somebody help? It's going to pull me in!'

He started laughing and grabbed the pole. 'It's okay, boy. It's not going to pull you in.'

Then he showed me how to turn the handle to reel in the fish.

'Now, nice and gentle. I'll hold the pole and you start reeling this bad boy in.' He looked at me. 'I think you might have just caught us some supper tonight, boy.'

I turned and turned the handle, pulling in the line and bringing what I was sure was some monster of a fish that had lived on the bottom of this pond for 62 years. It was hard, but I kept reeling it in.

'Come on, boy. You can do it. You almost have it in now.'

Then I felt a tug and the reel went spinning. I held onto the pole tight.

'What's happening? Help me!' I looked at Uncle Dan and panicked.

'It's fine. That fish is just trying to make a run for it. Here, let me help you.'

He did something to the rod and then told me to start slowly turning the handle again. I did, and felt the fish trying to swim away. I thought maybe that fish was stronger than me, and that I wouldn't eat fish even if there was no bacon on the entire earth.

He got a net ready to scoop up the fish when it got close enough to the boat. And then, suddenly, before I could really even figure out what was going on, I saw a giant fin sticking out of the water and then Uncle Dan reached out and pulled up this big fish that looked like a shark right into the bottom of the boat.

'Oh my God, boy, it's a catfish. And a big one. I was sure we were going to catch a bream today. Pepper, you did really good. We are going to eat great tonight.'

I jumped up on my seat, so that the fish didn't bite me. It had what looked liked whiskers hanging off its mouth. And I thought that maybe there were rows and rows of teeth on this baby shark.

'Boy, sit down. You're going to tump us over.'

I shook my head no. The boat kept tipping back and forth, and, though I kind of knew how to swim, I had never been swimming in a lake before. Who knows what else was down there waiting to eat me up?

'Sit.' He held the fish with one hand and put the other one hard on my shoulder. 'Sit, Pepper. Or at least squat. Otherwise we're going for a swim.'

I squatted down. I didn't know how to swim very good. I could dog paddle, but didn't know my strokes yet. I was supposed to learn those this summer at swimming lessons. And I definitely didn't want to be in the water with more of these giant fish with fins like knives.

'Is it a shark?' My insides were shaking against my ribs.

'No,' he said, pulling the line straight. 'It's a catfish, like I said.'

'It looks like a shark.'

He laughed at me. 'It's not. It's a catfish, and good eating right there.'

He wound the line around one hand and put the other one under the fins so he could look into the fish's mouth.

'Shit. It swallowed the hook.' Uncle Dan yanked on the line and the fish started wiggling and blood poured out of its mouth. Uncle Dan jerked back and dropped the fish.

'Damnit,' he yelled. 'Stupid fish got me right on the thumb.' Now Uncle Dan was bleeding too.

The fish fell to the bottom of the boat, and started flipping all over the place. Drops of blood spotted my shorts and legs.

I stood up again. 'Awwwwwwww.' I screamed. This fish was going to stab me. I just knew it.

Again, the hard hand on my shoulder. 'If you don't sit down, Pepper. I'm going to…'

He stopped himself as he heard a voice from the side of the lake.

'Dan. Dan!' A man in a red baseball cap on a four-wheeler waved his hands in the air. 'Hey, man, it looks like ya'll caught some dinner. What'd you catch?'

Dan tried to grab the fish with his one hand again, and pushed me down into the bottom of the boat. 'Catfish,' he said. 'The fucker got me with its dorsal.' He gritted his teeth.

The guy laughed. 'Well, hold it up and let me see.'

'Oh, man. I kinda got my hands full here.'

'You can't catch a fish in the bottom of your boat? What kind of wuss are you?'

Uncle Dan sighed. 'I can catch the fish. I'm catching the fish. If you would just shut up and let me concentrate for a second.'

The guy on the shore turned off the four-wheeler.

'Who you got with you?'

Uncle Dan sighed and wiped his forehead on the sleeve of his t-shirt. 'My nephew, but he's kinda shy, so we're just going to finish up fishing.'

'Your nephew? Did he come for a visit or something? I want to meet him. I didn't even know you had a nephew. My John would probably love to play with him. What's he, like, six?'

I looked up at Uncle Dan. If he didn't get this right, I was going to be mad.

'He's eight. He's just little for his age. See you later, Phil.'

Phil stood there for a minute, his hands on his hips. 'You know I ain't leaving 'til I get to meet your kin, Dan. Bring him over. I'll wait on you. I want to see that fish too.'

Dan sighed and grabbed the catfish and shoved his hand into its mouth. 'Jesus. I just wanted to catch some fish.' He pulled out the hook, finally, and, with it, some of the fish's guts.

Quickly, he threw the fish into a Styrofoam ice chest behind him. I could hear it flipping around inside. He put his hand into the lake to wash it off, then stuck the side of his thumb in his mouth.

Phil had gotten off his four-wheeler and stood on the side of the lake. 'That one got you, didn't it!'

'Yeah. Just a minute. I'm coming over.'

Blood poured down Uncle Dan's hand. He tore off part of his t-shirt and wrapped his thumb in it. Under his breath, he said, 'People just can't leave you alone sometimes. Makes me crazy.'

I squatted in the bottom of the boat, afraid to move, and watched the red water swirl around my shoes. There were holes in my shoes, and the blood water was running into them, leaking onto my feet. Uncle Dan's thumb kept bleeding through the rag he had wrapped around it. He needed a Band-Aid. I mean, he really needed a Band-Aid. I thought he might bleed to death if he didn't get a Band-Aid soon.

'You need a Band-Aid,' I said, head down, watching his hands as he tried to start the engine. They were shaking again, like they did in the truck. It was like a lawnmower. He kept pulling this handle with a string on it, but the engine wouldn't start.

'Shut up, Pepper,' he said, in a whisper. Then he stopped pulling and waved to his friend on the shore. 'Sit the fuck down,' he whispered, teeth clenched, 'before you fall out of the boat.'

I sat down, my lips zipped. I didn't like Uncle Dan's hands, and I knew I didn't want to make him mad at me. Plus he was cussing, and I knew from my momma that when she cussed she was really mad. And he said the f-word. That was the worst word you could say.

He took a deep breath and pulled again on the pull cord. Finally, the engine sputtered awake. Within just a minute, we were at the edge of the lake and Uncle Dan was all smiles again.

'Hey, Phil. How are ya?'

'Pretty good, except for my back keeps giving out. Hurts like a son of a bitch sometimes. Sounds like you need new spark plugs. Did you check them before you went out this morning?'

Uncle Dan stepped onto the bank, and directed me to follow him. 'Come on, boy.' I jumped out of the boat as fast as I could. I hated that bloody water touching my skin. He looked back at the boat. 'Yeah, no. Well, we were in kind of a hurry, so I didn't check them. I think they're okay, though. It just does that sometimes.'

The man looked at me. 'Well, hey there, boy. I'm Phil. You can call me Mr. Phil. What's your name?'

I looked down at my toes. It was just easier than trying to piece together all the pictures of the man's face. Uncle Dan elbowed me in the ribs.

'Cat got your tongue, boy?'

I looked at Phil's mouth. Mouths were easier for me than eyes. He had brown specks all between his teeth. I started counting them, avoiding his whole face for now.

'Pepper.' I stopped for a second. 'Uncle Dan needs a Band-Aid.'

Phil laughed. 'Pleased to make your acquaintance, kiddo. Pepper? What kind of name is Pepper?'

I looked at his teeth again. My momma said that if you can't look somebody in the eyes, stick to their nose or their mouth, because it made them think you were looking at them. 'It's my name. For me,' I said. Then I tugged on Uncle Dan's pants leg. 'Can we go fishing more?'

I didn't want to go fishing anymore. I just wanted to go inside and take a shower. I was already covered in 389 blood speckles, which looked like freckles on my arms and legs. And I couldn't even see the ones on my face to count them, but I could feel them there, drying up.

'Hold on a sec, boy. I just want to get to know you. I got a boy about your age. John. Well, he's nine already, and he loves to go hunting with me during deer season. You ever hunt, boy?'

I shook my head no.

'Well, you can hunt with us some time if you want.'

I didn't want, so I just stood there and watched his hands.

He put one of his rough fingers under my chin and lifted it up toward him. I closed my eyes so that pictures of his face wouldn't confuse my brain so much. 'Boy, didn't anybody ever tell you you're supposed to look at folks in the eyes when they talk to you? Otherwise, they'll think something's wrong with you.'

He let go of my chin and I looked at my arm. Even with the blood speckles there, I was pretty sure nobody would think I was a raccoon. I just looked like a kid who had killed a fish. And raccoons were smart. Mean, but smart. I wasn't sure that Phil knew what he was talking about.

He paused for a second, then looked at my head. And up at Uncle Dan. 'Boy, what happened to your head? Dan, he's got a huge lump on his head? Did he fall?'

'No, we had a little incident in the truck the other day. The kid went right into the dashboard. He's okay, though.' I kept my head low and watched Uncle Dan's shaking hands.

'Better out than in, I always say. Still, you might want to get a doctor to check that out.'

'You think? He's a pretty tough kid. He'll be fine in a few days.'

He scrunched up his face and looked at Uncle Dan again. 'Is. He. A. Little. Slow. Or. What?' His mouth moved like he was talking to someone who spoke a different language.

'Shut up, Phil. The kid ain't slow. He just don't like talking to stupid people.' He punched Phil in the stomach, but not too hard. 'You know what I mean?'

'Hmmmm. Okay. Well, you taking him back home today? It's Sunday. I mean, he does go to school and all, right?'

Uncle Dan started messing with the rag he had wrapped around his thumb. His hands were still shaking. I was beginning to think there was something wrong with him, like he had the shaky hand disease. 'Man, my thumb's killing me. That catfish really got me.'

Phil turned his head sideways and spit something brown onto the ground. 'Yeah, I want to see that catfish. It looked like a big one.'

Then he said, 'So, how long is the kid staying? I want to bring John over if he's going to be here a while.'

Dan looked up and fixed his baseball cap. 'Yeah, I mean. Sure. He might like to meet John. He's kinda shy, though, don't talk that much.'

'Yeah, I figured that out. How long's he gonna be here, though?'

'A while. We're still working all of that out.'

'Huh? What do you mean? Whose kid is this? I met your brother that one time, but he had all girls.'

'Oh yeah, this is my sister's kid, my little sister's kid.'

'You never even mentioned you had a sister. Where does she live?'

Uncle Dan paused for a second, so I spoke up. 'In heaven.'

Phil took a step back and sucked in his breath, coughing on the brown stuff in his mouth. He looked at Uncle Dan with a funny look on his face.

'He means Nashville. But...' Uncle Dan stopped for a second and looked down at the ground, his hands still shaking, if you looked closely at them. 'She passed suddenly the other day. It was a surprise for all of us. They called me, well, because Pepper here didn't have anywhere else to go.'

He was wrong about that, though. I had Sabrina and Christopher. And Mimi and Papa. And I even had Uncle Meanie and Aunt Vicky, and 27 first, second, and probably even third cousins, plus a great-aunt and a great-uncle. I had lots of places to go, but none of them had made a promise to my momma to take care of me, except for Uncle Dan.

'Dan, I'm so sorry. I had no idea, man.' Phil grabbed Uncle Dan's shoulder and held on for a second. 'I wish you'd told me, so I could do something for you.' He paused. 'If nothing else, I could've brought over a case of Bud and we could've looked at some old family pictures or something.'

Uncle Dan wiped his eye, like he had an eyelash stuck in it or something. It was probably blood from the fish. 'Thanks,' he said. 'It was all so fast. There was an accident, and they called me. Plus, you know, I don't like making my burdens other people's business.'

Phil took a deep breath and looked back at me. 'Well, Pepper. It looks like we're going to get to be good friends after all. You're going to love my John. He'll teach you how to catch rabbits, ride a four-wheeler, and maybe even shoot come deer season.'

Phil started walking toward his four-wheeler. 'I'll bring John over tomorrow after school.' He stopped and turned back toward us. 'Hey, where are you going to school, Pepper? Maybe you and John could ride on the bus together. He'll show you around and all.'

I didn't answer, so he looked at Uncle Dan.

'I assume he's going to Oscar Hamilton, right?' Phil added.

'Uh yeah. I guess. I mean, he just got here Friday. We haven't really gotten everything settled just yet.'

Phil smiled. 'Welcome to fatherland, Dan. The truancy officer will be out here soon enough, so you might want to get him registered some time this week, you know?'

Uncle Dan looked down at the ground. He wasn't looking at Phil in the eyes either. 'Yeah. I got this. This ain't my first rodeo. I mean, how hard can it be?'

Phil made a clicking noise and laughed. 'Wait until you have to help him with his homework. Those weekend projects will kill you.' He spat again and got on his four-wheeler. He started it up and drove off.

'Shit,' Dan said. 'We gotta get your birth certificate together for school.'

Chapter 4

We spent the next week going to the doctor's office, where I got a shot in my leg; going to Walmart, where I got a new Plants vs. Zombies backpack, lunch box, and a bunch of school supplies; and the Sonic, where I got chicken strips, french fries, and a chocolate milkshake. Uncle Dan lied about the doctor's office. He told me I didn't have to get any shots. I told him that I hated doctors, that I wasn't going to get out of the car, that doctors hurt people, and I had been to way too many doctors. I knew what they did.

He grabbed my arm and dragged me into the sick-smelling office, one that smelled like Band-Aids and rubbing alcohol, where the lady sitting at the front desk smiled and asked my name.

'Pepper,' I told her, wincing at Uncle Dan's hand around my arm.

'Pepper what, hun?' She typed into her computer. I didn't respond. She looked up at Uncle Dan.

He squeezed my arm harder. 'Johnson,' he said. 'It's Pepper Johnson.' He looked down at the woman. 'I know, hell of a name. His mom was a little loopy from the anesthesia when she picked that one. But you know women… I wanted to let her have her way.'

The woman rolled her eyes. 'Is he a new patient?'

'Yeah. Just moved to town.' He stopped for a second and whispered. 'We had a sudden death in the family, but I do have his immunization records.'

'Great. Can I see those?' She scrunched up her forehead and continued to type into the computer.

Uncle Dan got a sheet out of his wallet. He had one of those wallets with a chain on it, so he didn't lose it.

'And why are you here to see us today?'

'Oh, well, we just need to get him a new immunization form, the one they use for school,' Uncle Dan said.

She sighed. 'Well, the doctor is going to have to see him then.'

She handed us a clipboard of papers. 'Fill out these forms.'

We sat down on the far side of the waiting room, and Uncle Dan chewed on the end of the pen while he filled out the forms.

I pointed to the top line. 'My last name isn't Johnson.'

'I know,' Uncle Dan gritted his teeth. 'But I had to put my last name on there so that you could use my insurance.'

I pointed to the next line. 'That's not my birthday.'

'Pepper, stop. You're driving me crazy. I'm doing the best I can.'

'Well, I should know when my birthday is. It's February 15. You didn't put February 15 on there. Can you change that? I want them to know when my birthday is. Maybe they send out birthday cards or buy you a Lego or something on your birthday.'

'Look, Pepper. I don't have time for this. Do you see all of this shit I gotta fill out?' His hands were shaking again.

'But, you have to do it right! It's really important.' My voice was getting louder and higher. I could feel my brain start flipping upside down. I tried to breathe, but I knew I was going to lose it soon. I focused on his hands, the cut on his thumb, the Band-Aid that was still bloody, the dirt under his fingernails, the way he closed them into fists, released for a second, then made a fist again.

He reached into his pocket. 'Here. You like phone games? Play a game on my phone.'

I felt my spinning brain slow down to its regular speed. 'I like phone games.' I grabbed his phone and tried to unlock it. 'It's locked, Uncle Dan. Can you help me?'

He kind of growled at me, but entered a code into the phone that opened it. 9822. I would remember that number without even trying.

I checked out the games on his phone. 'You have Angry Birds? I love Angry Birds!'

He put his face down close to mine and whispered, all mean like into my ear. 'No dialing the phone. No calling anyone. You hear?'

I looked up at him for a second.

'I mean it, Pepper. You dial anyone and no games.'

'Okay, no dialing. Yes, Angry Birds.'

I got on Angry Birds and played it for the 15 minutes that it took Uncle Dan to fill out the papers. When he went to take the clipboard up to the woman at the desk, I flipped over to the number part of the phone. I knew how to dial on a cell phone. My mom had one and, when I was little, I would dial people all the time just to hear them say, 'Hello? Hello?' Sometimes they would get mad that I didn't respond, but that was when I didn't talk, so I wasn't being rude, I had lost my words and couldn't find them again for a couple of years.

It looked like Uncle Dan's phone worked just fine. I wondered why he didn't want me dialing. Maybe he thought I would call Hawaii or New Zealand or something. I wanted to call home, but knew I would have to wait until another time, when he wasn't around.

Uncle Dan came back and sat down with me, peeking over at the phone. I was fast. I was already back on Angry Birds and on level seven.

'You any good at that game?' Uncle Dan asked.

I nodded. He laughed.

'You had a lot of practice, huh?'

I nodded again, then focused on trying to knock down all of the bricks with the red bird.

'Pepper Johnson.' A lady with green scrubs on called my name.

Uncle Dan grabbed the phone, took me by the hand, and walked me through the door.

The doctor took this bright light and looked in my eyes, blinding me, so that I could only see spots; my nose, which tickled; and my ears, which he said were perfect. He made me follow the light with my eyes without turning my head. Then he looked at the bump on my forehead. It was mostly gone, but I still had a big bruise that was turning yellow around the edges.

'That's some bump you got there, young man. How did that happen?'

I didn't answer because I didn't like talking. I didn't like doctors, and I especially didn't like talking to doctors.

Uncle Dan spoke up for me. 'He's kind of shy, that one. But we had a car accident last week. Poor kid banged his head pretty good on the windshield.'

The doctor turned to Uncle Dan. 'He can't ride in the front seat until he's twelve,' he said. 'And, even then, he has to wear a seatbelt.' His face got red and his voice sounded mean.

Uncle Dan paused for a second. 'Oh, I know. That was the problem. I have a truck, and we were driving along and he took his seatbelt off. I was trying to get it buckled back up when this car stopped really fast right in front of me.'

The doctor sighed and turned back to me.

'I stuck out my arm to try to catch him, and I almost did, well, except for his forehead, which hit the dashboard.'

I didn't think the doctor believed him either.

'I thought you said the windshield,' he said.

'Yeah, that's what I meant.' Uncle Dan stammered on his words, which I could understand. That happened to me all of the time. 'I mean, it was the dashboard, not the windshield. He's too little to hit the windshield. And I wasn't even going more than 30 miles an hour.'

The doctor pressed on my bump, which was less like an egg and more like a little hill now.

'How does that feel, Pepper?'

I didn't want to talk to him at all, so I kept my mouth shut.

'Pepper, tell the doctor how your bump feels.' Uncle Dan looked at me mean behind the doctor's back. 'Tell him now.'

I looked up at the doctor's face. He seemed like an okay guy. But I knew I was going to have to get a shot or something. 'It's okay. It doesn't really hurt anymore. Not even when I move my head around.'

The doctor looked into my eyes with his eye viewer thing again. 'Not when you move your head up and down? Or side to side?' He moved my head around as he talked.

'Nope. It's all better now.'

'Do you have any headaches?'

I wasn't really sure what he was talking about, but 'no' seemed to be the right answer.

'If something like that happens again, you need to bring him in. He could have had a concussion.' The doctor looked at Uncle Dan. 'Do you understand?'

'Yeah, sure. It really wasn't that bad. Just a little bump. It looks a lot worse than it was.' He paused for a second. 'There wasn't even any bruise there until yesterday.'

I looked at Uncle Dan's face. I wanted to remember what it looked like when he lied. Then I would know when he told me the truth and when he was lying.

The doctor told me to lie down and he undid the snap to my jeans.

'So, now we have to take a look at your privates. Pepper, do you know that nobody but you or your parents are supposed to touch your penis?'

I just looked at the doctor. He pulled down my pants and pushed at the bottom of my stomach and around my private area.

'Nobody means nobody, okay?'

I nodded my head and wondered if nobody meant him.

He pulled my pants up and smiled at me. 'Okay, kiddo. You look pretty healthy to me, but you let me know if that bump starts hurting again.'

He turned to Uncle Dan, who wiped his forehead on the inside of his t-shirt. 'Okay, so let's get him a flu shot and we'll have you out of here with your school forms as fast as we can.'

Uncle Dan sighed and slouched down in a chair after the doctor left. 'Kid, you're going to be the life of me, I swear.'

I wasn't sure what that meant, but I was mad that I had to get a flu shot.

I was limping through the Walmart, because the flu shot hurt my behind. I hated shots. And why did they always have to give it to you in your behind? I had no idea why doctors couldn't figure out how to give medicine in some other way, like in lollipops or gummy bears. They put vitamins into gummy bears. I knew because my mom used to give them to me every morning. Two. Usually red and yellow. But I hated the orange ones, and if she put one out I would sneak it into my pocket and trade it with somebody at school who thought it was a real gummy bear and not a vitamin one. Why couldn't they put the flu shot into a gummy bear? That would probably taste terrible, but, still, it would be better than getting stabbed in the behind with a giant needle.

I didn't cry, though. Mostly because Uncle Dan told me I couldn't get a Plants vs. Zombies Garden Warfare backpack and lunch box if I did.

When we were at the doctor's, Uncle Dan had held onto my arm so hard while I was getting the shot that I was more worried about him breaking it than the shot. He did this thing when he got mad where he clenched his fists until his knuckles turned white. I knew better than to act up when he did that. I didn't want him hitting me in the head again.

We went down the aisle with all of the chips. I asked Uncle Dan if I could get some popcorn.

'You like popcorn?' he asked.

'Yeah. Don't you like popcorn?'

'Yeah, Pepper. I like popcorn.' He leaned down and grabbed a box of the microwave kind. 'Kettle or Movie Butter?'

I looked at him funny. 'Movie Butter.' I was thinking, who eats Kettle? Barf. 'I know how to make that kind myself,' I told him. 'My momma taught me how.'

I thought about my microwave at home and started to worry. What if Uncle Dan didn't have the popcorn button like we did at my house? Then I wouldn't know how to make my own popcorn. My breath caught in my chest, my feet stopped walking, and I started moaning a little. 'No, no, no, no, no.'

My brain started flipping over and over, like it was going to spin out of my head. It felt a little better when I hit myself on the head with my palm.

'Jesus, kid. What's wrong now?'

I didn't answer him, and just kept saying, 'No, no, no,' over and over again. I was starting to cry.

Uncle Dan bent down in front of me. 'Look, Pepper. You've got to stop doing all of this crying bullshit.'

He grabbed my arms and held them down by my side. 'And quit hitting yourself in the head. Shit, kid. You're way too smart for that.'

He got up close to my face. 'Stop crying and breathe. Take deep breaths and hold them in for a second.'

My momma used to do that. She would get up close to my face. I could look at her eyes then, like these big oceans of blue swimming in front of my face. I could lose myself in her eyes. And she would breathe really loud and slow, saying, 'In through your nose; out through your mouth. Fresh air in; pain out.' She would stay like that until the weight fell off my shoulders and I wasn't choking on the air anymore.

But Uncle Dan's eyes weren't blue. They were brown, like mine, and he didn't know how to do the breathing thing like Momma did. Plus, my momma never held my arms down hard like Uncle Dan did.

Then he told me what he said was a joke. 'You ever try crying in the shower?'

I just looked at him and tried to remember my mom's face as she breathed. I didn't know the answer.

'It's impossible. There's too much water and you can't figure out what's your tears and what's your shower water.'

I smiled, since he said it was a joke. It didn't sound like a joke to me, but I knew I was supposed to laugh at jokes.

'Now,' he said. 'Tell me what you want. A different kind of popcorn? One with cheese on it or something? The one in the purple box? What is it?'

I looked at him in the eyes, even though I didn't like doing that; it took too much attention to hold the pictures together for even a few seconds.

'Do you have a popcorn button on your microwave?'

'What? What are you talking about?'

'On your microwave. Is there a button that says popcorn?' I needed to know. I was about to start crying again. I felt my chest get tight with sobs that wanted to come out so bad.

'Um, well. I don't know, to tell you the truth. I haven't really looked at it that close.'

'Oh no, no, no, no.' I started again, hitting myself on the head with my palm.

'Pepper. Cut this shit out. Right now!' His voice was hard and loud.

He grabbed my hands again and took a deep breath. 'Okay, look. Here's what we'll do. I bought my microwave right here in this Walmart. Let's walk over to the microwave section and we'll find the one I bought and see if it has a popcorn button.'

I thought that sounded like a good idea. I breathed like my momma taught me. My head quit spinning around and my chest loosened up some. I wiped the tears on the top of my arm, leaving wet streaks all the way down to my fingers.

He grabbed my hand and we started walking toward the appliance section.

'And, Pepper. Even if it doesn't, I'll teach you

how to make popcorn so that you can have it any time you want. Okay?'

I looked up at him. 'Huh?'

'I'll teach you. It's no big deal. You can make popcorn any time you want. I'll show you how. You don't have to have a popcorn button.'

I understood him the second time.

'Thanks, Uncle Dan. That's why I was crying.'

'No more crying, kid. If you have a problem, before you start freaking out all over the place, you come to me. You ask me. I'll fix it for you. That's why I'm here, you know?'

After we found Uncle Dan's microwave, which did have a popcorn button, we headed toward the school supplies section. I was so excited when I saw they had the Plants vs. Zombies Garden Warfare backpacks with matching lunch boxes right there on the shelf. And they were so cool. They had these Plants vs. Zombies Garden Warfare tags that looked liked somebody had taken a bite out of them, plus a zombie on the front of both the backpack and lunch box.

I start jumping up and down. 'Plants vs. Zombies Garden Warfare! Plants vs. Zombies Garden Warfare!' I pointed to the shelf.

Uncle Dan didn't even know what that was. I had to tell him all about it.

'You can get it on your phone. I used to play it on my mom's phone. It's so cool. I'm on Day Level, but I'd really like to get to Pool Level. If you got it on your phone, I could play and show you how too.'

We were standing in Walmart, looking at the backpacks. Uncle Dan said one word, 'No.'

I was still jumping, on my tiptoes, trying to keep my excitement inside of my body.

'Oh come on, Uncle Dan. It's just one game. And it's the coolest game ever.'

He just looked at me. 'Quit asking me for so much stuff. I'm getting you the backpack and lunch box for school. I'm pretty sure you don't need another phone game.'

'But you can play too. You'll love it. It's really fun. I have 10,879 coins, 23 weapon upgrades, and I've killed 4,087 zombies. I'm at level three as a Peashooter. Actually, he's a Gatling Pea. Snapdragon is pretty good to have too. He shoots fire out of his mouth, over and over, at all of the zombies. And I'm a five-star on the Sunflower. I like Chomper the best. He's really the best player. And I've killed all kinds of zombies: conehead zombies, buckethead zombies, football player zombies. And it's so cool! You gotta get it on your phone for me. Come on, Uncle Dan.'

I was jumping up and down. I was so excited. It was the most fun game ever. He got this really mean look on his face, and said the one word that I dreaded more than anything: 'No.' Then he added. 'Stop asking about it. I said no.'

I started to cry, but he put his hand hard on my shoulder again and I knew I better not. I wasn't sure if he was going to hit me or what, but I wiped big, long streaks of tears down my arms and sniffled the snot back up into my nose as he grabbed the backpack and the lunch box and we headed toward the check out line. I reminded myself not to ask for candy today, even though my body wanted sugar so much.

Anyway, I knew that I just needed to get his phone a few more times. I knew his passcode, and I was pretty sure I could figure out his iTunes password. I mean, I needed Plants vs. Zombies, and Uncle Dan's phone was the way to get it.

Chapter 5

The next day, Uncle Dan drove me up to the Ash Grove Cafetorium at Oscar Hamilton Elementary School. I wasn't sure what a cafetorium was or who Oscar Hamilton was, but I knew what elementary school was, and I didn't like it one bit. You had to get up early, sit in your desk all quiet, try to keep your behavior clothespin at an 'E' for excellent (like an 'S' wasn't good enough and I knew Uncle Dan would get mad), and do extra homework when you got home. There was no cable tv, no video games, and somebody was always telling you that you were doing something wrong. And the noise. I don't know what it is about kids, but they yell and scream like nobody's business. Plus, they pick their boogers and don't understand why you push them away when they try to hug you.

Uncle Dan opened his door and told me to get out of mine. He had an envelope with the papers from the doctor in it plus my birth certificate. I knew, because I had peeked at it the night before. My last name was wrong on it, but at least the Pepper part was right.

He held my hand as we walked into the big building that said 'Cafetorium' in big white letters. It looked like a nice enough school, all red bricks, so nobody could blow it down. I was pretty sure it was the strongest building I had ever been in. I tried to start counting the bricks the minute I got out of the door of the car, but Uncle Dan was walking fast, so I only got up to 237 before he got me into the door. The building smelled and looked new, not like my old school, which had stairs all over the place and missing tiles on the floors. This one had colored tiles that alternated every third one with an off-white tile, blue, yellow, red, green. I would have to count each one eventually, but, as soon as we walked in the door, there were kids running everywhere, old ladies yelling at people where to go, and parents trying to fill out papers. It was like they were all yelling in my ears at once. I squatted down on the third green tile that I saw. Green is my favorite. I got tiny, so that the noise couldn't get so close to me, and squinched up my eyes and pushed my hands hard over my ears to shut it all out. I wasn't going to cry or yell, because I knew Uncle Dan would be mad at me, but that noise in there made my breathing all rattly again and my brain start spinning over and over on top of itself.

I was trying really hard just to be little and not make a fuss, but I wasn't sure how long I could squat there. I started edging off my square in little, tiny steps toward the door. It was going to take me a while, but I could get there eventually without letting go of my ears or standing up.

Suddenly I felt a swoop, and then I was still in a little ball, but tucked into Uncle Dan's hoodie. He zipped up the front of his jacket so that it was all nice and dark and then headed toward the door with big steps. I could feel his arms around my back, holding onto me so that I wouldn't fall out. His heart beat fast into my ear, one, two, one, two, one, two. It made me feel like I was alive and safe, counting his heartbeats over and over. He kept walking until he got to the office, where it was quiet, so I looked out of the top of Uncle Dan's hoodie. One old lady with cat eye glasses sat at a big green desk. She unwrapped a mint and popped it into her mouth before asking, 'Can I help you?'

'Yes,' said Uncle Dan. 'We need to get my son, Pepper, here registered for second grade.'

I had already done second grade, or at least most of it, and here he was, putting me in second grade again.

'Registration is in the cafetorium.' She said the word 'cafetorium' slowly, as if Uncle Dan didn't understand English. 'And why is your son under your jacket?'

'See, that's the problem. We went to the cafetorium.' Uncle Dan didn't stumble over that word, so he must have known what it meant. 'It's too noisy in there.'

I peeked out of the hoodie again. The lady looked confused.

'Too noisy for what? It's registration.'

Uncle Dan held onto me tightly. Then he unzipped his hoodie and I unfolded out and stood next to him. He wiped his forehead on his sleeve. 'It's too noisy for him,' he said, pointing to me. 'And for me too. Hell, it's too damn noisy for anybody in there.'

'I'm sorry, but that's where you'll have to go to register him. Are you new to the district?'

'Yeah. He is.' Uncle Dan paused for a second, then smiled so big that I could see his gold tooth again. 'Listen. Pepper here has some noise problems. Things get real loud for him real fast.'

The old lady nodded.

'I'm sure you understand. It's going to be impossible for me to take him back in there, and I can't leave him sitting out in the truck. Did you read about that little girl that got fried because her momma left her sitting in the back seat of their car while she went gambling?'

The old lady's mouth moved into an 'O.'

I looked back at Uncle Dan, who looked at the lady like he had just told her the best secret ever.

'Yeah, right. So, I can't do that. And I'm a single dad.' He waited a second and put his hand on my shoulder, only gentle this time. 'I'm doing the best I can here.'

I looked up at him. From the way his voice

cracked, I thought he might start crying. I put on my sad face, thinking that was what he wanted me to do. I was sad, sort of, but mostly just scared to be in this place with so many people, so many lights, so much noise.

'Can you help us out and let us fill out the paperwork in here? Then maybe you could just give it to the principal or whoever is in charge of registration, so my poor kid doesn't have to suffer like that little girl?'

I glanced over at the old woman. She looked like she was going to cry then. She got a Kleenex and spit her mint into it, then stared first at me and then at Uncle Dan.

'You poor thing. Sure, honey. Here's the paperwork and you can sit down right here and fill it out. I'll make sure Mrs. Foreman gets it. Do you have all of your proper identification and his immunization forms?'

'Yes. I think we have everything: utility bill, lease on my house, his birth certificate, his social security card, and the blue form from the doctor.' He pulled a bunch of papers out of the envelope. 'I think that's everything, right?'

She smiled and handed me a mint. 'Here, honey. Have a mint while your daddy fills out those forms. It cleanses your breath.'

I didn't tell her that he wasn't my daddy. I just took the mint and unwrapped it, slipping it into my mouth. I imagined that it was like a scrub brush, cleaning away my bad breath while I sucked the sugar out of it. My brain was happy again.

Three days later, Uncle Dan drove me back to Oscar Hamilton Elementary School. On the way, he reminded me that my name was Pepper Johnson, even though I knew it wasn't. It's Joseph Phillip Branigan, officially, I reminded myself. I wouldn't forget it, no matter how many times he told me my name was Pepper Johnson. Most everybody called me Pepper, but nobody had ever called me Johnson. What kind of name was Johnson? My last name was Branigan. But, by then, I knew better than to tell him different, though. I smiled and nodded so he would think that I believed him that I was Pepper Johnson. Everybody could think I was Pepper Johnson as far as I was concerned, as long as I knew the truth. I kept repeating my real name over and over so I wouldn't forget though. One day I would need to know the truth, so I imprinted it in my head to help me remember.

We drove up to the red building with the white letters, the one that was rough on your fingertips when you ran them along the bricks. I had to wear khaki shorts and a white shirt with itchy tags. I wanted him to cut them off, but I hadn't thought about it until we were in the truck. And Uncle Dan didn't keep scissors in the truck. He had bought them for me at Walmart, so they were brand new.

He didn't even wash them before I put them on, which my momma would have a fit over. I didn't like it either. They smelled like dye and I was sure it was seeping into my skin in every place that they touched me.

This time I got up to 541 bricks before he moved me toward the door. I had learned to count fast. We walked back into the office and saw that same lady with the glasses sitting behind her green desk. This time, she didn't give me a mint, but smiled at Uncle Dan and handed him a piece of paper that had my homeroom and teacher's name on it. I read it over his shoulder. I knew what a homeroom was, but I didn't know who Ms. Drozinsky was. I wasn't even sure I could say that, but I could read it on the piece of paper. Ms. Drozinsky, Grade 2-02, Room 103. I saw those numbers in my head, 103, imprinted them there, just in case I got lost.

Uncle Dan stopped in the hallway outside of the office. 'It's just down there, on your left,' he said. 'Just look for 103. You'll be fine.'

I stood there and looked at him.

'You've got your backpack and your lunch box. It's got your lunch in it, just the way you like it: a cheese stick, Goldfish, a green apple, and a Hershey's bar. I'll pick you up after school right outside these doors.'

He had only figured out what I liked for lunch after he had asked me the day before. I was mad that I didn't tell him Slim Jims. I loved the way they tasted so salty and meaty, but my momma didn't like me eating them, because they had 'too much sodium,' she said. I didn't buy that, because I loved them so much, but she only let me have them when we had to drive a really long way in the car.

I looked down the hallway. Lockers slammed. Kids screamed. Boys ran. Girls laughed. The bell rang and everyone scattered. It was loud, and the noises crept toward me like ants, running up my legs and arms, stinging when they bit into my skin, marching straight into my ears and moving into my brain faster than I could think. I shook my head to try to get them to clear out, and held onto Uncle Dan's hand, so he wouldn't leave. As far as I could see, nobody else had a Plants vs. Zombies Garden Warfare backpack. What if they didn't even know what Plants vs. Zombies Garden Warfare was? In the past two days, I had downloaded the game onto Uncle Dan's phone, using his iTunes password. I was pretty sure he had no idea what any of the icons on his phone meant, so he would never know about the $3.99 it cost. So, I knew I was smart. I could do things, especially with electronic things. But this place? This place was scary. Too many kids, just like zombies, running around like crazy.

'It'll be fine. Just walk down the hall and go into room 103. On your left.'

My feet were stuck inside of a green tile, and they weren't moving.

'Pepper,' he sighed. 'Go.' He pulled his hand away from mine and started to walk toward the front door.

I looked at him, panicked, but he kept walking. I squatted down and shut my eyes, putting my hands over my ears again. Maybe it would all disappear if I squeezed my eyes hard enough. Maybe I could get very, very tiny and disappear into the green square that both my feet were standing on. Maybe the zombies would just come and get me and I would be re-spawned on top of a house, or at my old school, or any place far away from all of these kids.

It seemed like I was there for ages, but maybe it was only 15 very long minutes until I heard, 'Shit,' as Uncle Dan picked me up and carried me under one arm, like a football, down the hall. I stayed in a ball as he walked. He was taller than all of the kids, so I just sailed over their heads until he put me on the ground in front of room 103. There was a sign on the wall that said, 'Welcome, savvy second graders. Ms. Drozinsky.'

I leaned up to Uncle Dan's ear. 'What's savvy?'

He looked at me kind of funny. 'It's like you, super smart and all.'

Then he bent down, his face at my level. 'Now, here's the deal. You're Pepper Johnson, the smartest kid in this room. Get in there and show them how amazing you are.'

I thought that he was lying again. He lied a lot, and I wasn't sure what to believe.

He opened the door and Ms. Drozinsky smiled really big. I looked down at her shoes, red ones with little black stitches all over them. I started to count them, zooming in on each stitch that ran around the strap of her left shoe.

'Hi! You must be...' she stopped and looked at me.

I looked up and smiled back, because that's what my momma said you're supposed to do when people smile at you.

Uncle Dan put his hand on my shoulder, this time hard again. 'Uh, this is Pepper. Pepper Johnson, my boy.'

'Well, Pepper. I'm glad you've decided to come to Oscar Hamilton Elementary. I think you're going to love second grade here.'

I looked at her neck. It was the closest I could get to her face. I could tell her face was beautiful, but I couldn't look at it just yet. She had this tiny gold cross on a chain around her neck. My mom wore a silver one with smooth edges that she had bought at Tiffany's when she was 16 years old, the first thing she had ever bought with her own money, she told me. I wasn't sure who Tiffany was, but I used to rub on that cross when I was little and the world seemed too big and too loud. Red shoes and a cross like my mom's. I liked Ms. Drozinsky already.

Uncle Dan patted me on the head. 'Look, Pepper. I promise I'll pick you up out front at three o'clock. You're gonna have a great day.'

I grabbed Uncle Dan's hand and pulled his ear toward me. 'Promise you won't leave me here for forever,' I whispered in his ear. He might have been a liar, but he was all I had.

He smiled, his gold tooth shining in the back. 'I promise. I'll be right out front. Three o'clock.' He pointed up to the clock, then turned to walk away. The big hand was on the six and the little hand was on the eight. I knew that meant 8:30. Three o'clock seemed a long time away.

'You better be there so you can play Angry Birds on my phone, okay?'

That made me smile. I counted the twelve steps he took, walking away from me. I was not completely convinced that he would come back. 'Okay. I'll be there.' And I'd be playing Plants vs. Zombies, not Angry Birds.

He looked at Ms. Drozinsky before he walked out the door. 'He's quiet, but super smart. Wait until you see him do math. He's a genius.'

Then he opened the door and shut it behind him. And I didn't see Uncle Dan again until the big hand was on the twelve and the little hand was on the three.

I looked around the room. There were six chalkboards on two walls, three bulletin boards on another wall, then the last wall had eight windows running from corner to corner. Each window had two parts, one on the top that you couldn't open and one on the bottom. All of the bottom ones were open, and I could feel the air as it tried to suck the heat out of the room. There were nine perfect window panes in each section. I counted them quickly. That was eight times two times nine. 144. I started counting the tiles on the floor, some were blue and some were white, when Ms. Drozinsky interrupted me.

'So, Pepper. Why don't you choose which desk you want?'

I looked at the desks. There were four desks pushed together to form a square table. There were five tables altogether. That was 20. I counted the kids: 19. 38 eyes, all looking at me, plus two with Ms. Drozinsky's. I put my chin on my chest and looked down at my shoes as they walked me over to the desk at table four, the only seat that wasn't already taken. There's not a lot to pick from if there's only one. I wasn't sure this school was going to work out for me.

I had to sit with three kids, two girls and a boy: Destiny, Zoe, and Rashad Prince. I had never heard of anyone with the name of Rashad Prince. I was pretty sure that he was a prince of somewhere. He had the tallest hair and the blackest skin I had ever seen, and a gold front tooth with a white star on it. I wanted to look at that tooth all day long. I wondered if he was related to Uncle Dan and my mom too. Watching his tooth was much easier than listening to Destiny and Zoe, who talked without stopping, telling each other what boy liked what girl, and what they did the night before. I had to cover my ears for the first ten minutes of class and concentrate on Rashad Prince's tooth before I could make my ears ignore their words.

Ms. Drozinsky was really nice, but her name was next to impossible to pronounce.

'You can call me Ms. D., if you like,' she said, but she wrote the whole thing in cursive on the board, the big 'D,' the 'z,' which kind of rolled off the 'o' and into the 'i,' then the curly 'y' at the end, which kind of held her name up in the air, like an arm.

I kept saying it over and over in my head, though. I would practice it until I could say it. I knew I'd need to know her whole name someday. Ms. D. wasn't going to be enough. I kept looking at the letters, their curves, trying to print them into my brain, so I wouldn't forget them. But, every time I looked down at my paper, the letters, her name, just disappeared into the air like smoke. I focused. I knew I could do it. Finally, I converted her letters to numbers. Numbers, I knew, would stay: 4, 18, 15, 26, 9, 14, 19, 11, 25. Drozinsky. There.

She put spelling words on the board and told us to write them down. I wasn't very good at writing. It was hard to get the words to stay on the line and sometimes letters jumped over each other. But I wrote down the ten she put on the board anyway: 'lean,' 'learn,' 'earn,' 'bean,' 'clean,' 'dean,' 'glean,' 'mean,' 'wean,' 'churn.' I had no idea what 'dean,' 'glean,' and 'wean' meant. And why was 'churn' in there? It didn't even have an 'ea' in it. She made us write sentences that included each word.

1. I learn my spelling words.
2. I earn a bean if I clean up my room.
3. Uncle Dan leans down to churn the butter.
4. He is mean.

I just wrote 'dean,' 'glean,' and 'wean' at the bottom. And hoped she wouldn't notice.

She came over and looked at my paper. 'Put your name at the top, Pepper.'

I wrote 'Pepper.'

'Your whole name, honey.'

I wrote a capital 'B,' but then froze. I checked to see if she was watching me, which she was, then I erased it. Uncle Dan wouldn't like that. His strong hand might hit me again if I wrote Branigan.

'It's Johnson,' Ms. D. said. 'Do you need help with that?'

I looked up at her.

'Big J.' She waited while I wrote it. It was weird putting someone else's name next to Pepper. 'o-h-n-s-o-n.' She stood there until I finished, then put her soft hand on my shoulder. 'Don't worry. You'll get it.'

I think she thought I was dumb, that I didn't even know how to spell my own last name, but I did: B-r-a-n-i-g-a-n. No need for numbers for that one. My mom had told me every day when we walked to school. Joseph Phillip Branigan. And no matter what Uncle Dan told me, I wouldn't forget it.

After spelling, we did math, and I got to write on the board, showing everyone how good I was at adding and subtracting. I wrote the problem as clearly as I could, then wrote down the answer. I was the first to finish and just knew she would be impressed. I could multiply too, but we didn't get to that yet. Maybe that was next week.

I sat down at my desk, and Ms. D. said, 'Pepper. You need to show your work.'

I wasn't sure what she was talking about. I had written both numbers, one on top of each other, and the answer at the bottom. I looked at her.

'On the board, honey. Show your work.'

I looked down at my lap and hoped she would call on someone else. Everybody else was still up at the board. She walked over to me. I could feel her standing next to me. She leaned down and I could see her gold cross dangling in the air on its chain out of the corner of my eye.

'Pepper, do you know what it means to show your work?'

I nodded yes. She smelled like flowers and our front yard right after Christopher mowed it in the spring. I wondered if he was still mowing the grass. And where, since he couldn't live with Momma anymore either.

'So, will you go up there and show the class how you got your answer so fast?'

I shrugged.

'Can you show your work?'

I shrugged my shoulders again and looked at the board. I had. Couldn't she see it?

She leaned down to whisper to me. 'That's a complex sum, Pepper, a three-numeric subtraction problem. How did you know how to borrow without writing it down?'

I looked at the cross. 'I don't know. The numbers just appear in my head.'

I could feel her smile. 'Really? Just like that? That fast?'

I nodded.

'Hmmmmm,' she said. 'That's very good, Pepper. Your daddy said you were good at math. We'll try some more problems later. I'd like to see you do more in your head.'

I smiled, because I think I made her happy.

'You like math, Pepper?'

I nodded again.

'Good. More math later.' She looked toward the board. 'Granger, borrow from ten's place if you can't subtract that seven from the one.'

She put her hand on my shoulder, and I tried not to flinch. She seemed nice, but I would watch her to make sure.

We had lunch, where I ate everything in my lunch box and tried to drink the blue Gatorade in the Thermos that he put in. It was like drinking liquid salt, but I didn't want him to get mad at me, so I poured what I couldn't finish into the garbage can. Nobody talked to me at lunch, but that was fine, because I was busy trying to count all of the blue floor tiles, which was tricky with all of the tables in there and kids running around. I liked recess the best, where we played kickball on the playground and I could finally breathe the air. It was so much better than sitting down in a classroom all day long.

After recess, we went back inside for science and social studies. Ms. D. gave me my book, but told me that it was 'to remain at school in my desk.' I wasn't sure why we couldn't take the book home, but I stared at the cover. It said *Know Arkansas* at the top. She told us to turn to page 42.

But as I was looking for page 42, I saw that there was a map of the United States and one of Arkansas in the front cover of the book. I saw Tennessee on there and Memphis right in the left hand corner. I raised my hand.

'Yes, Pepper?'

'Where are we?'

'Oscar Hamilton Elementary, Pepper. I know it's confusing, but you'll get the hang of the school in the first few weeks. Do you need to go to the bathroom? Ricky can show you where it is.'

I shook my head.

'But where are we?'

'What do you mean, hon?'

'Like Tennessee? Are we in Tennessee?'

'No, Pepper. Of course not. We're in Arkansas. Look at the title of the book. See? It's called *Know Arkansas*.' She paused for a minute while she closed the book and pointed to the title. 'And now we are going to learn about the native animals of Arkansas. Page 42, everyone.' She looked back at me on her way to the board. 'You too, Pepper.'

Arkansas, not Tennessee. I would learn everything I could about Arkansas so that I could get back to Tennessee and find my momma.

Uncle Dan did show up at three o'clock, just like he said he would. And he let me play what he thought was Angry Birds on his phone on the ride home. As long as I said 'Go, red bird' or 'Get him, blue bird,' he didn't know I was playing Plants vs. Zombies Garden Warfare. But, of course, the next day he dropped me off at school, just like the day before, and I had to do it all over again.

Chapter 6

By Friday of the first week, Ms. D. had given me seven math tests, sometimes with the class and sometimes when the other kids had music or library. I didn't mind missing library, but I loved music. I loved to sing. It was the only time that the words came out easily and I didn't have to think about them. I aced every test, and she gave them back to me with 100 and a big red smiley face on them, telling me, 'Math really is your thing, Pepper. I'm really proud of you.'

I would nod and look at my shoes or hers. Mostly hers. I only had one pair and had memorized every stitch in them, so I looked at hers. She hadn't worn the same shoes since the first day, so I made a chart with the shoe color, style, stitching, and heel of each one. I wondered if she had one pair for each day of the year, or if she would ever wear the same shoes twice.

'As good as you are at math, you might need some help with talking.'

I didn't look up.

'I know you're a good talker, but just a little shy. So we're going to give you a special friend who will stay with you all the time and talk to you. You know, extra practice.'

I thought she meant I would have a partner, like on field trips, but then she said that I needed to have a one-on-one to go to classes with me. Ms. D. introduced her as my 'new friend, Ms. Harrison.' I read the paperwork, upside down, on Ms. D.'s desk, and, even though I didn't know what 'ancillary attendant' meant, I was pretty sure that Ms. Harrison was it. That was okay, though, because as soon as I saw Ms. Harrison I knew I would like her. She had the darkest skin I've ever seen, even darker than Rashad Prince, and the whitest teeth. That first day, she walked into the class-room and smiled at me with those teeth. Then she said, 'Great to meet you, Pepper. I'm your new friend.'

I needed a friend, and she seemed like the perfect person to me. She was really skinny, but loved can-dy, and she was nice enough to share, even on that first day. So I had sugar pretty much every day. But the best part about Ms. Harrison was that when I finished my work early, she would let me play with her phone while she went to the bathroom or the teachers' break room to have a snack.

'I have low blood sugar,' she would tell me.

And I would nod back to her. I knew how it felt to need sugar.

Ms. Harrison made me work hard, but she smiled really big any time I did my math work. 'You're a math genius,' she whispered to me. I wondered if Uncle Dan had told her that. It was the same thing he had said that first day when he dropped me off.

Ms. Harrison went with me just about everywhere, except for lunch. She even went to PE, art, and library with me. It was pretty cool, because she would always have a sharpened pencil, or a mint in her pocket, and always, always, her iPhone.

I heard the factory default ding that nobody ever bothers to change. Text messages, I knew, because my mom had one too.

She put the phone in her lap and checked the text.

'I love Plants vs. Zombies,' I said.

She stopped mid-text and looked up at me. It was the first time I had spoken to her without her talking to me first. Her mouth made a little 'O' for a second. Then she smiled her white teeth back at me.

'Oh, you do, do you?'

I nodded.

'Well, I'll tell you what, if you finish that math sheet early, then I'll run get a snack and you can play Plants vs. Zombies on my phone. How does that sound?'

I wasn't sure if she was lying. Maybe she was like Uncle Dan and just lied sometimes. I narrowed my eyes at her. 'Plants vs. Zombies Garden Warfare?'

'Sure, Pepper. You can play anything you want.'

I started on the first problem. We were doing three-digit, four-number addition, which was easy enough to do in my head, but Ms. D. wanted us to show our work. I hated carrying the ones, then crossing out the numbers, and writing new ones above them. I could do these in my head a ton quicker, but Ms. D. insisted. She still wasn't convinced that I could do them without writing them down, even though I had shown her like 100 times. She kept trying to make the problems harder and harder, but my brain knew numbers so I kept doing them and trying to show her how to carry without actually writing it down.

'Do you have it downloaded onto your phone already?'

'Yep. I sure do. I play sometimes when I'm not at school.'

I went back to the problems. That was all I needed. I would be at number 20 in no time.

When I finished the page, back and front, she put the phone in her pocket and walked up to Ms. D.

'Ms. Drozinsky, Pepper's done with his math. Is it okay if he walks to the teachers' lounge with me for a second?'

Ms. Drozinsky nodded and looked over at me. 'Yeah. They said to take a lot of breaks with him, so he doesn't have a melt down. Walk him upstairs a few times too. Try to get his ya yas out.'

Ms. Harrison smiled at me. 'Come on, Pepper. We're going to get your ya yas out.'

I had no idea what she was talking about, but as soon as we were in front of the teachers' lounge she gave me her phone. 'Look,' she said. 'I'm just going in here for a few minutes, but students aren't allowed. Sit right here and play on my phone. You can play Plants vs. Zombies.'

She started to walk away. 'Seriously, Pepper. If you go anywhere, then I won't let you play on my phone anymore.'

That scared me. So, I promised. 'Okay, okay. I won't. I promise.'

She hooked my little finger in hers. 'Pinky promise?' She smiled really big at me.

I smiled back, because that's what you're supposed to do. 'Pinky promise.'

We shook on it and she walked into the teachers' lounge. I stuck my feet on the blue square underneath me and told them not to move. The door shut behind her, and I slid open the phone. I figured I had about four and a half minutes before she came out. It depended on how low her blood sugar was.

I thought about Plants vs. Zombies Garden Warfare for a second. I loved that game, and I was really good at it. Then I thought about my momma. I missed her. I decided to call her numbers to see if she would answer. I said them to myself every morning so I wouldn't forget: 373-1888. I hoped I wouldn't get in trouble. Maybe Ms. Harrison wouldn't even notice. I had to try at least.

I dialed them and the recording of the nice lady's voice came on. 'Your call cannot be completed as dialed. Please check the number and dial again later.'

Dang. I knew my momma wouldn't disconnect her numbers, not if she were still alive. I dialed her numbers again. Same lady. Same message. I pushed End. I almost started to cry. I just knew my mom was alive. And I knew her numbers. I just didn't know how to make her answer the phone.

That's when I saw this kid walking down the hall. He was little, but in the fifth grade, and I knew he was smart. People talked about how smart he was at lunch. He was the only kid I had ever met with white hair. He was one of the few people I could look at, mostly because I wanted to keep staring at his hair. I closed my eyes, and tried to think of his name. Johnathan? Jeffrey? Hank. Hank Absolom. What was he doing walking down the hallway all by himself?

'Pepper, right?'

'Yeah.' I blinked, trying not to let the tear creep over my eyelashes. 'Hank?'

He ignored me. 'You're that math genius kid, right?'

I nodded. 'Sorta.'

'Why are you crying like a baby out here? And who gave you that iPhone?'

I bit my lip. I was NOT a baby. I blinked away my tears, but worried they would start rolling out of my eyes and I wouldn't be able to control them. 'Ms. Harrison. She's going to be back in a minute.'

Actually in three and a half minutes. I was counting down the seconds in my head.

'You playing a game on it?'

I looked at him and wondered if I could tell him the truth. I didn't think I liked this kid, but I was sort of afraid he was going to steal Ms. Harrison's phone if I didn't say something.

'Well, really, I'm trying to call home.' I wiped my eye. 'But it's not working.'

'What do you mean? Give me that.' He snatched the phone out of my hand.

'Don't!' I said. 'Don't drop it.' I hit myself on the head. I was so stupid to give him Ms. Harrison's phone. Now she was going to get mad at me and never let me use her phone again. My knees shook as he held the phone in his hands.

'Chill, Einstein. My mom has an iPhone too. I've made like 1,700 calls on her phone before. Why are you calling home? You forget your lunch or something?'

I didn't answer him and he didn't really pay attention to me. He started typing into the phone. Three minutes.

'Man, she's got some great games on here. Did you see Monster 500?'

I nodded. 2 minutes 50 seconds.

He hit the bottom button and showed me his phone.

'Oh, yeah. See, here's the thing. You don't have enough numbers.'

Two minutes thirty-two seconds. I looked at him confused. 'What do you mean?'

'You only have seven. You gotta have ten.'

He showed me the screen, which said Recent Calls at the top. 'See, right here? You need three more at the beginning of the number. It's called the area code.'

I looked at the seven numbers that I had there. That was all my mom ever wrote on my arm. That was all of her numbers. She didn't have anymore. Two minutes.

'Try putting three numbers in front there.'

I didn't have anymore numbers to put in front of them. I tried to tell him, but my hands got all sweaty and my mouth got dry. I had to hurry. I was running out of time. He gave me the phone back and started to walk away.

'What numbers?'

'Hey, I don't know. My mom's are 870. But my aunt up in Little Rock has 501. Try those.'

He stopped three feet away, and walked back. 'Here's the thing, though. If you're going to make secret phone calls on someone else's phone, you have to delete the number so they don't know.'

I just looked at him.

'Give me the phone, retard.'

I scowled at him, but he didn't look at me. He grabbed the phone and showed me the screen. 'Look. After you make a call, just swipe it to the side, like this.' He moved his finger across the screen over the last call I had made to my mom. 'Swipe it to the left. Then hit the delete button and no one will ever know you made that call.'

I squinted at the screen.

'See? The call disappears. Just like that.'

I nodded as he walked off. Ninety seconds.

'Work on the genius part next time, dude,' he said, before he rounded the corner.

'Thanks,' I whisper yelled, not wanting to get in trouble, but wanting him to hear me.

I tried 18 more numbers, each time putting different combinations in front of 373-1888. I got seven recordings where the woman told me I had the wrong number, all in a row. Then I got three voicemails. 'Hi, this is Sandy. I'm not able to answer my phone at the moment. You know what to do.' I knew what to do, but didn't know anyone named Sandy. I hung up. I got five more recordings telling me the number I had called was not in service, and to please check the number and try again. I tried again. Two more voicemails: one for a man named Jimmy. Another that just gave the number. On the eighteenth call, a lady answered.

'Hello?' she said.

'Momma?' I asked. She didn't sound like my mom, but it had been two months, so maybe her voice had changed.

'Yeah,' she said. 'Whose phone are you using?'

I was pretty sure it wasn't my mom. 'The lady who helps me do my work. Her name is Ms. Harrison.'

'Uh, who is this?'

'Momma?'

'Justin, listen. If you're playing a trick on me, this isn't funny. Is there something wrong with your phone?'

I wasn't sure who Justin was, but this wasn't my momma. 'I don't have a phone.'

'Wait. I think you have the wrong number, kid. Are you playing with your mom's phone or something?'

'No, I'm trying to call my momma.'

'Well, this isn't her number, so you're going to have to hang up and ask somebody for her number. Okay?'

I paused, not knowing if I could tell her to come and get me or not.

'You okay, honey?'

'Yeah, I guess,' I said. 'I'm just trying to get home.'

'Well, call your mom's number and she'll come and get you.'

'Okay. Thanks.'

Then she hung up. I swiped delete on all 18 calls just as Ms. Harrison came out of the teachers' lounge.

'You get to any new levels?' She smiled at me for a minute before I knew what she was talking about. 'On Plants vs. Zombies. Or were you playing Angry Birds?'

'Oh yeah. Plants vs. Zombies.' I looked down at my feet. 'Nah, I got stuck. Maybe you can help me?'

'Me? You're supposed to be the genius, kid. Likely you're going to have to help me.'

I was beginning to think that genius was what I would try to be, smart enough to get back to my momma.

That weekend, Uncle Dan and I went fishing again. I didn't mind it so much anymore, because he let me drive the boat lots of times. But I still didn't like it when he caught the fish. The smell of the blood almost made me throw up. And I never, ever ate one of the fish he caught. But that's how he liked to spend his weekends, he said. And when he asked if I liked spending my weekends that way too, I nodded. I knew better than to say no.

On Saturday night, after we had been fishing all day, Phil knocked at the door. I don't think Uncle Dan expected him, because he was watching football highlights and drinking his fourth Miller Genuine Draft. His voice got angry when he heard the knock.

'Go into your room and don't come out until I tell you to.' He looked at me with his mean eyes. I could see the veins on his neck pop out. I wasn't sure what I had done to make him mad.

I nodded and walked in my sock feet across the den to my room. I shut the door and lay on the bed, counting the boards in the ceiling. I had done this every night to go to sleep, but it also helped my brain when the grumpy switch turned on.

I heard Uncle Dan talking really loudly. 'Hey,

Phil. You surprised me. I didn't know you were coming by, man.'

I could hear Phil's voice through the crack under my door. 'Oh, I just thought I'd bring by a six-pack and see what you're up to. You catch any fish today? Smells like you cooked something up tonight.'

I turned off the light in my room and cracked the door so I could see a sliver of Uncle Dan and Phil. I made sure that I breathed in real quiet, long and slow, so they wouldn't hear me.

Uncle Dan yanked on the waist of his jeans. They still had blood on them from the fish he had caught that afternoon. 'Yep. Well, you know me. I'm pretty good with a rod.'

Phil held out the beer. 'Well, you gonna invite me in or make me stand in your doorway all night?'

Uncle Dan took the beer, but his feet didn't move. 'This a housewarming present or what? I've only lived here for 17 years. Hell, Phil, these ain't even cold.'

Phil edged around Uncle Dan, whose feet remained planted. 'Yeah, sorry about that. They been sitting in my truck all day. I just wanted to check on you. Make sure everything was okay with the boy and all.'

Uncle Dan flashed Phil a big smile. 'You know, it's good. We're still getting used to each other, but he's in school now and doing okay.' He stepped out of the doorway. 'Come on in. I got an ice chest full of cold ones right here in the den. We can watch the highlights from today.'

'You watching the game?' Phil asked as they moved toward the den.

I cracked the door a little wider so that I could see them better. I got on my stomach, and started to inch my way down the hall, toward the den.

They talked about football for 18 minutes. I counted it off in my head. I slithered on my stomach, ninja style, until I was under the kitchen table. I steadied my breathing again after I slid into the shadow of the table. 1, 2, 3, 4 in. 1, 2, 3, 4 out. 'Even breathing,' my momma called it. Nice and slow and quiet. Then I curled up into a ball. I could be really small when I wanted to. I decided that being small was a good thing, something that came in handy, like when I was trying to overhear people's conversations.

Phil asked for another beer, which Uncle Dan opened with one bare hand before giving it to him. His hands were strong. I didn't like them.

'So, how's it going with Pepper?' Phil asked, looking at Uncle Dan.

'Oh, the boy's fine. He's a math genius, I tell you.'

Phil's face didn't change. 'My boy, John, says he has a lady who walks around with him all day.'

Uncle Dan took a big sip of his beer and ignored what Phil had said. 'Oh, John's seen him at school? Pepper didn't even mention it.'

'Who's the lady, some kind of helper or something?'

'Nah, man, that's nothing. Just a way for the public schools to spend our tax money.'

Phil wasn't buying it. 'John says she's from Africa.'

Uncle Dan seemed to choke on his beer. 'Africa? That girl ain't from Africa. Sure, she's dark. She's real dark. But she's smart as a whip. They're giving him extra work, because he's so smart. She's there to try to help the other kids in the class who can't keep up.'

Phil nodded.

'Why you believe everything your nine-year-old tells you anyway? He's not even in the same grade as Pepper.'

Phil took a swig this time and swallowed before answering. 'My John tells the truth. He's no liar.' He put the beer on the coffee table, where it clanked, and rubbed his hands on his jeans.

'Yeah,' said Uncle Dan, 'but how good is he in math?'

'Oh, you know. We aren't the best in math at my house. He goes to pull-out to get extra help. But he's okay. He's making Cs at least.'

'Well, Pepper's doing better than a C. I'm sure he's making all As, especially in math.'

Uncle Dan looked back at the tv. His face was blue from the reflection. He and Phil were quiet for twelve minutes and two more beers each. This time when he talked, Uncle Dan was slurring his words, like he had a mouthful of cotton.

'I love that kid. I gotta tell you. I don't know what I would've done if I hadn't gotten him.'

Phil looked down at his work boots and wiped his mouth. 'Yeah, I know, Dan. I love my John, too. Sons are the best, aren't they?'

Uncle Dan clinked Phil's bottle. 'It's been a long time since anybody thought about me as their Daddy.' I noticed that Uncle Dan's hands were shaking again when he put the bottle to his mouth. 'I'm just trying to do right by my sister.'

'I know you are. And you're doing a damn fine job of it too. I mean, you got him into school, and he's out there fishing with you, and, from what I can tell, the kid's not covered in mosquito or tick bites, even though it's September. I'd say that makes for a pretty fine daddy. You going to teach him how to shoot when deer season starts?'

'Yeah. I mean, maybe. The kid's not too much of a fisherman, so we'll see. Not sure I trust him with a gun yet.'

I stuck my lip out. I thought I was pretty good at fishing. I could drive the boat and all. They were both quiet for the three whole minutes I counted off in my head in Mississippis.

'I miss mine, though. You know? My boy, Bo.' He wiped his eyes and put his beer up to his forehead, pushing his baseball cap back when he did.

I caught my breath. Bo? Who the heck was Bo?

Phil bit his lip. 'Yeah. That was some sad business.' He stopped for a second. 'Where'd she end up anyway?'

'I don't know. West Virginia was the last I heard.'
Uncle Dan moved the cold bottle to his cheek, like
he was really hot and needed it to cool him off. 'I
miss my Bo, and I'm afraid I'm never going to see
him again.' He wiped his eyes. 'Stupid bitch. She
always was mean as a snake.'

Phil took the last swig of his bottle. 'Hand me
one more, bubba.' He paused. 'It ain't right her running off and not letting you see your own flesh and
blood. I mean, that can't be legal even if she did
cross seven state lines.'

Uncle Dan opened a beer and passed it to him.
He flicked the bottle cap toward the wood-burning
stove. 'I ever see that woman again, I'm going to let
her have it. It ain't right and it ain't legal. But I can't
afford a lawyer, so I'm pretty much screwed.'

They both looked into their beers like they were
trying to see inside the bottles.

'How old would Bo be now?' Phil asked.

'Would be? It's not like he's dead or nothing.
He's eleven. Got a birthday on November 30.'

Uncle Dan's eyes looked like they might leak at
any minute. I had never seen him cry. I figured it
out. Bo was his son, like me, only his real son. Why
would anyone take away your son?

'No reason to wallow, though,' Phil said. 'You got
to keep your chin up and just thank the good Lord
that you got Pepper. I mean, I hate that your sister had
to go and die and all, but you got a son again, man.'
Phil swallowed again. 'That's something right there.'

'Yeah. You're right. Pepper is pretty strange, but he's a good kid.'

I wondered what he meant by 'strange.' Was it because I hated loud noises? Or because I didn't like it when the blood splattered on me in the boat? Or that eggs made me gag? My momma always said that we liked 'weird' in our house, but I wasn't sure if 'weird' was the same as 'strange.'

They drank for a few more minutes, the tv flickering on their faces, until Phil asked, 'So, do you miss her?'

'Jenny Anne? Why would I miss her? I haven't seen that bitch in ten years. I stopped missing her about nine years ago. I hate that stupid bitch.'

'No, man, your sister. I didn't even know you had a sister, but I'd think y'all were close if you inherited her kid.'

Uncle Dan took a sip of his beer and wiped his upper lip with the back of his hand. 'You know, sure. I miss her. I mean, we haven't spent a whole lot of time together in the last few years, other than Christmas every now and then.'

I sucked in the air as quiet as I could. I knew that was a lie. Uncle Dan had never been to Christmas at my house. I would remember him if he had. And I had never been to this house before. I would remember what gift he had given me. I knew every birthday and Christmas gift that anyone had ever given me. And not one Lego, Skylander, or Angry Bird plush toy had ever come from Uncle

Dan. I felt my face get hot. I counted to 369 by threes until it didn't feel red and mad anymore.

'Yeah, I got a sister up in Oklahoma City. I haven't seen her in five years. I'm gonna have to make a point to get up there some time soon.' Phil paused. 'She's got five kids. God forbid anything happen to her and I have to take care of all of them. That would do me right in.' He chuckled and Uncle Dan did too, even though he kept wiping his eyes.

It was that night, while I was lying under the kitchen table, listening to Phil and Uncle Dan talking over football, that I realized it. Uncle Dan wasn't my uncle and my momma was still alive. She was probably looking for me every single day. I had to figure out the first three numbers to put with the other seven that I knew were my momma's numbers. And then I had to dial it without Uncle Dan knowing. I slithered on my belly, ninja style, back to my room, as Uncle Dan and Phil started talking again. I climbed into bed and stared up at the ceiling tiles, counting them until my breathing slowed down and my brain stopped being mad. I decided right then and there that I would keep trying numbers until I figured it out.

Chapter 7

At school the next day, when the big hand was on the four and the little hand was on the ten, my teacher looked at the clock and called my name. 'Pepper, come up to the front of the room for me.'

She was standing there with another lady I had never seen before. I wondered if I was in trouble for counting the floor tiles again. 124 blue. 124 green. 148 red. 174 yellow. And the rest were white. I couldn't count all of the white ones because the rug and Ms. D.'s desk covered lots of them. I had gotten up to 439 white ones.

I looked at Ms. D. until she called me again.

'Come on, Pepper. You're not in trouble. I want you to meet someone.'

I walked to the front of the class and the other lady, who was short with dark brown hair, shook my hand. 'Hi, Pepper. I'm Ms. Adama. I'm a speech therapist. You're going to be working with me three times a week, okay?'

I nodded my head. I wasn't sure what a speech therapist was.

'So we'll go down the hall to my office, where we'll work together.'

I looked at Ms. D. to make sure it was okay. I swear, she could read my mind sometimes. 'It's okay, Pepper. You can go with her. She'll bring you back in time for recess.'

I looked at the side of Ms. Adama's face. She was pretty, and had brown eyes and a mole right over her lip. My mom used to call that a 'beauty mark' when we saw one on tv. She had dark eyebrows that made her look like she was mad most of the time, but a smile that reminded me of my momma. She took my hand and walked me down the hallway. I felt a catch in my throat, like my breath was stuck there. I realized that nobody, except Uncle Dan, had held my hand since I had been at That Amazing Pizza Place, and that was Rosalind Jane, whose hand was sweaty. My heart sat down at my feet, because it hurt so much missing my momma. But I liked Ms. Adama's hand. It was smooth and felt like a cloud against mine. I was pretty sure I would like Ms. Adama.

'So, Pepper. Ms. Drozinsky tells me that you're good at math. Really good at math.' She looked down at me, but I kept my eyes on the floor. I was counting the tiles in the hallway, which was my favorite place to count tiles, because there wasn't any furniture in the way.

I nodded.

'Why do you like math?' she said, twisting the

key to her classroom, which, as it turns out, was more like a closet than a real-sized classroom.

I shrugged.

She told me to have a seat in the red chair at her little table. She had four colors of chairs. I really liked green better, but did as she said. She sat in the blue chair next to me. She looked too big sitting in that chair made for kids. There was a basket of pencils on the table, all blue, yellow, green, and red to match the chairs.

'What does this mean?' She shrugged her shoulders like I had.

I shrugged again.

'You, Pepper, are a man of many words.' She got her phone out. 'You like Angry Birds?'

I looked at the phone, then up at her face. I nodded.

'No more nods. You have to use words.'

I didn't really like words, but I wanted to get on that phone. For the Angry Birds and to call my mom.

'Yes.'

'Yes? That's it? You must not like them all that much if "yes" is all you can give me.'

I thought about it. I remember my mom telling me to look people in the eyes and speak very clearly when I talked to them. That way, she had said, I could get what I wanted, at least some of the time.

'Yes. I love Angry Birds.' I talked slowly and looked at her brown eyes. 'Now can I play on your phone?'

She laughed. 'It's going to take more than two sentences to play games on my phone, kiddo, but yes, if you do good today, I'll give you five minutes at the end. Deal?'

'Deal.'

She put her hand out and shook mine.

She started asking me all sorts of questions. I knew the answers to most of them: what was my favorite color (she let me sit in the green chair after I answered 'green'), what was my favorite tv show, why I liked math. 'Because the numbers just appear in my head.'

'Appear?' She scrunched up her face like she didn't understand.

I stopped and looked into her eyes again. 'Like magic. I just see the problem and poof.'

'Poof?'

I nodded.

'Can you do that when you hear problems instead of seeing them written down?'

'Sometimes. If I write them in my head, then the poof comes.'

'Huh.' She made some notes. 'I like magic math.'

'I like numbers.'

She smiled. 'Will you tell me why?'

'Because. They never lie. They always tell the truth.'

Then she asked me what my full name was.

It's a trick question, I thought. I reminded myself of what Uncle Dan said. I needed to be careful how I answered. I waited, counted the seven buttons on her shirt, then the stripes that went across them, 39, then started on the stitching on her shoes. Stitching was my favorite.

'Your full name is...?'

I frowned. I had to get this one right. I knew it was important, but how would my momma ever find me if she was looking for Joseph Phillip Branigan and I was Pepper Johnson, because Uncle Dan renamed me?

'Pepper Johnson,' I lied. I wasn't even sure it was a lie, but it felt like a lie after hearing what Uncle Dan had said to Phil.

'Good job, Pepper Johnson.' She put her face up close to mine. 'Now what's your middle name?'

Uncle Dan hadn't covered this one. I didn't know what to tell her. It was Phillip. I knew it was Phillip, but I wasn't sure if I was allowed to say it. So, I shrugged.

'You don't know your middle name? Or are you just tired of talking?'

I took a deep breath, like my mom told me to do when I got stressed, and started counting the green pencils.

'Come on, Pepper. My job is to get you talking. I want you to practice talking here with me, then we will go out and talk to other people, like teachers and your classmates, and all sorts of people.' She paused. 'But you gotta start here. Tell me your middle name.'

I looked at her face and decided to take a chance.

Surely she wouldn't tell Uncle Dan. She probably would never even meet Uncle Dan.

'Phillip. It's Phillip.' Twenty-seven green pencils.

She smiled. 'Of course it's Phillip. That's where you get the nickname Pepper from, right?'

I shrugged.

'No shrugging,' she scolded.

'Yeah, I guess. I don't really know. I've been Pepper forever.'

'I'm sure you have, kiddo. You look like a Pepper to me.'

Then she just looked at me for a minute. I guessed she was thinking about what a Pepper looked like. I didn't know what a Pepper looked like, but I figured it was me. Like my mom said, it was a special name, and only for me.

'So, what do you like to do when you're not at school?'

I looked down. I liked to call my mom.

'I don't know.'

'Yeah, you do, Pepper. I'm sure you and your parents do all kinds of fun things on the weekend.'

She didn't know about my mom. Or my Uncle Dan. Thirty-two red pencils. I looked away again. I needed to get to her phone.

'We fish. In the lake.'

She nodded and smiled. Her teeth were nice and white, like my momma's. I wondered if she had a gold one too. 'Do you catch any fish?'

'Yes.'

'Come on, Pepper. What kind of fish?'

I thought about it. 'Ones that get blood all over the boat and me.'

Her eyes got big. 'Did you get hurt?'

'No. Almost. It hurt Uncle Dan.'

'It did? What happened?'

'The fish's fin cut his hand really bad. He needed a Band-Aid. There was a lot of blood and I don't know what was from Uncle Dan and what was from the fish.'

'Good job, Pepper. I want to hear more.'

I stopped. I didn't know what else to say. I'd told her everything. I mean, not about the worms and the crickets, but that part wasn't even important.

'Sometimes Uncle Dan lets me drive the boat in circles around the lake.'

'He does? That sounds like fun. I've never driven a boat before. I think I'd like to try that someday.'

I wasn't sure if she meant she wanted to try it with Uncle Dan and me or someone else. I looked at her shoes and started counting the stitches again. When I got to 98, she interrupted me.

'You live with your Uncle Dan?' Her forehead scrunched up all wrinkly.

I froze, smile plastered on my face. Then I looked at her and nodded.

'No nodding.'

'Yes. I live with Uncle Dan.'

'Is he nice?'

I looked at her eyes. I didn't like to lie. My momma always told me not to lie, but here was this lady asking me questions. I was sure she wanted the truth. But Uncle Dan told me his truth and that wasn't my truth.

'Mostly.'

She started making notes in her folder. I couldn't read them upside down, but they didn't have any numbers in them.

She looked up and smiled. It seemed like she didn't want to smile, but did it anyway.

'Tell me some of the things he does that's nice.'

I tried to think of something. 'He makes me bacon and lets me watch cartoons.'

'Oh yeah? What's your favorite cartoon?'

'*Pokémon*, I guess. I like *Phineas and Ferb* too, though.'

She smiled. '*Pokémon* and *Phineas and Ferb*. That sounds good to me.'

She scooted her chair back and made some more notes in her folder. 'Okay, Pepper. This is a great first day. I've really enjoyed getting to know you. Here's how things will work with us from now on.'

She told me that she would meet with me three times a week for 30 minutes. She said that we would talk in her classroom, and, on Fridays, we would walk around and talk to other people. She said, 'We can ask them about their weekends, and you can talk about what you're going to do on the weekend.'

I wasn't so sure I wanted to know what other people did on the weekends. I was stuck with Uncle Dan and fishing until I got that phone call in to my mom. I watched her clock until it was 10:55. I knew that meant we had five minutes left. She kept asking me about what I liked to do, what movies I liked, and why I liked math (again), which I tried to explain.

'Because, it's all even and logical. It makes sense. You can add numbers up, multiply them, subtract and divide, and you always get the same answer. It's either right or wrong. And if it's wrong, you just start over and try again until you get it right. And numbers never lie.'

'Good,' she said. 'Now, can you look at me when you talk about math?'

I looked at the top of her nose, like Momma told me.

'Yeah, I mean. I think I'm done talking about math.'

'Okay. What do you want to talk about now?'

I looked at the clock. We were down to four minutes. 'Can I play Angry Birds on your phone?' I looked at her face again, trying to put the 52 pieces of the puzzle together to make one. Then I smiled my best puppy dog smile, just in case she liked dogs.

'Okay, Pepper. That's what we agreed to. You can play with my phone while I fill out this paperwork.' She slid the phone across the table.

I knew I had to fool her. 'I love Angry Birds. It's the coolest game ever. Do you have Angry Birds

Winter? It's pretty awesome.' I opened the Angry Birds app, then went straight to her text messages. She had messages from 87 different people. 'Actually, all of them are awesome. I'm on level ten. What level are you on?' Why didn't she delete any of these messages? There were tons there. 'Which is your favorite? Red bird, white bird, yellow bird? I like red bird.' I started looking at the area codes on her phone. She had 570, 251, 601, 615, 876, and 398. She was texting people from all over the place. I took those numbers, plus a whole bunch of others, and put them in front of my momma's numbers and started sending texts. I knew I could get it right eventually.

I kept talking so that she would think I was playing the game, which wasn't easy to do when you were trying to text. 'Don't you wonder why they are all angry? I mean, they spend their whole day flying through the air hitting objects to get points. That would make me really happy, not angry.'

I sent 32 texts in four minutes. She had Siri, so it was fast. They all said, 'Hey Mom. I know you're still alive. I miss you every day. I love you.' Then I deleted them before Ms. Adama asked for her phone back.

'You must be good at that game,' she said, pretending to look at my success. 'You got to level three that quick?'

I knew she wasn't looking at my game. I never even played it. I wondered why she was lying, though, pretending to be looking at my game when she wasn't. I was too busy texting my momma. Surely one of those texts had gotten through to her.

Ms. Adama told me to stand outside of her classroom for a minute while she made a call. I hoped that when one of those people texted her back it would be my mom.

I counted the blue squares in the hallway, my eyes on the floor. It was my least favorite time of the day. Kids were moving through the hall, going to lunch. They were yelling and slamming lockers, and dropping their lunch boxes and books with a bang on the floor. I crouched down, trying to disappear from the noise. Then I felt someone poking me.

'Hey, Einstein. Why are you sitting on the floor? This floor is sick gross.'

I looked up to see a shock of white hair. Hank Absolom. I stood up and smiled at him. He was holding his Plants vs. Zombies lunch box. I wanted to tell him that I liked it, that I had one just like it, but I knew I had to talk to him quickly.

'I need something.'

'Yeah, genius? Like what? A new iPhone? You break that other one?'

I shook my head. 'No.'

'What do you need then? Hurry up. The line's moving. We're going into lunch.'

'The three numbers, the area code.'

Hank thought about it for a second while the girl behind him shoved him forward to catch up with his class. He stumbled, then let four people go ahead so he would be back near me.

'For where? You gotta know where?'

I was pretty sure of my answer. 'Memphis,' I said. 'Memphis, Tennessee. Can you get that?'

Hank smiled as he moved with the crowd down the hall. 'I can get anything, Einstein. All you have to do is ask.'

I wasn't sure why Hank Absolom wanted to help me, but I sure was glad. Ms. Adama opened the door and took my hand, tucking her phone into her pocket before leading me back to my classroom for recess.

Uncle Dan seemed to be a mind reader. When he picked me up from school that day, he opened the truck door, then said, 'So, I heard you got yourself a speech therapist.'

I shrugged, not really sure what to say.

He slammed the door, a little harder than he really had to, then jumped in on his side.

'There something wrong, boy?' He wasn't being mean, but his hands were shaking again. I never knew what that meant.

I shook my head.

'Your teacher told me it's because you don't talk enough in class.'

I counted the lines on the road as he drove out of the parking lot.

'So, you don't talk in class?'

I shrugged again. I talked. I answered lots of questions about math. They didn't require talking. Ms. D. just had us go up to the board and write the problems there.

'Look, boy. You gotta answer me. Don't you talk in class?'

486, 487, 488, 489. Lots of lines needed counting. 'I talk.'

'How much?'

'I don't know.'

'Pepper. What's the deal? How come you don't like talking?'

490, 491, 492, 493, 494. I loved the way 494 looked, so even with the 4s like bookends.

'People talk too much,' I said. 'They could talk a quarter as much and still be okay.'

'So maybe you need to talk more. Why don't you talk more?'

I thought about it for a minute. 495, 496, 497. I knew that at 1,089 we would be home, but that was a long time from here. 'People don't ask me questions that I like.'

'Pepper, what does that mean? What kind of questions do you like?'

I knew this answer. 'I like questions about Angry Birds and Plants vs. Zombies. I like questions about math and sometimes science. I really like ones about the planets. One question I really liked was: Did you know that Pluto used to be a planet and now it's not? I mean, how can they just change that out of nowhere?'

He laughed. 'Okay, I get it. I'll try to ask you questions about stuff you like so that you can practice. Do you like questions about *Phineas and Ferb*?'

I nodded, then broke into the theme song.

Uncle Dan's smile cracked his face again. 'Yeah, I know, Pepper. You like to sing, but don't like to talk so much.' He thought for a second. 'So, what kinds of questions do you not like?'

I knew this answer, but wasn't sure if he wanted to hear it. So, I shrugged again.

'Enough already with the shrugging. If you don't know something, say, "I don't know." And if you do know the answer, then answer. Don't be lazy, kid.'

He had on a blue plaid shirt with his sleeves rolled up. I wanted to count the lines, the squares, all of the colors in that shirt, but I didn't like looking at Uncle Dan for that long.

'So,' he started again. 'What kinds of questions do you not like? I'm not going to get mad at you or anything, but I don't want to ask you something you don't want to answer. Help me out here.'

'Okay.' I breathed in deep. I was at 691, getting close to Uncle Dan's house. I wasn't sure I could stall any longer. 'I don't like questions about stories we read. Those are boring.'

'Got it. I won't ask you questions about any stories, but you're a good reader, you know.'

I nodded. 'Yeah, but they make you read a story, then they make you take a test about it, then they ask you a bunch of questions and try to get you to say things that aren't even in the story. Sometimes they stop in the middle of a story and try to get you to guess what will happen next. I hate that. It's super boring.'

I flinched at the word 'hate.' My mom would say, 'Hate is a strong word.' Uncle Dan didn't flinch though. He asked me even more questions, like he didn't get that I didn't like talking.

'What else?'

'Um, well, I don't like questions about what I do on the weekends.'

'Why not? Don't you like what we do on the weekends?' He turned on the air conditioner, which blew Arctic air in my face, but felt good anyway. 'Man, it's hot as hell in here.'

I didn't answer. I thought maybe he would forget about it if I were quiet enough.

Then he remembered. 'So, the weekends? What's the deal? You don't like fishing?'

I thought about it. 'I don't know. I mean, yeah, it's okay. I don't like the blood from the fish. I like driving the boat, though. And I like watching football with you.' It was the third lie I had told that day, but it made him smile.

'Good. I like watching football with you too. I mean, what's Saturday in the fall without football?'

The lying part was getting easier every time I did it.

'And?' he asked. 'What else don't you like being questioned about?'

'My name.'

His hands shook just for a second before he steadied them by gripping the steering wheel. 'Who asked you about your name?'

'I don't know. People at school. Kids. Teachers. The principal asked me once.'

'And what did you tell them?' His voice was shaky when he asked.

'Well, I tell them what you told me to tell them. That my name is Pepper Johnson.'

He sighed. 'Good, Pepper. That's right. You're my son now, and your name is Pepper Johnson.'

897. We had two more minutes before we pulled into our long driveway.

'I have a question for you,' I said, looking at Uncle Dan's blue hat, the one he wore when he rescued me from those bad kids at That Amazing Pizza Place.

'Okay. Ask away.'

I bit my lip. 927. One more minute until we were home. I was afraid, but I was going to ask him anyway. I was scared he might hit me like he did that first night, but I had to know. 'Is my momma in heaven?'

He turned into the drive and my counting stopped. There were no lines on the gravel drive, just the crunch of the wheels on the rocks below them.

He grimaced and said, 'Yeah, Pepper. I'm sure your momma's in heaven. She was a good woman, and she loved you a lot. I feel certain that she's up there in heaven looking down on you right now.

But for me, I like to think that she's on a nice long vacation, like to Europe or somewhere in the Caribbean, you know, one of those islands like on the satellite tv. It makes me feel better somehow.'

That was his second lie, at least that I knew of. Nobody knows what goes on in heaven, so how could he know my momma was there? I was sure she wasn't in heaven. I was sure she was in Memphis, Tennessee, probably at That Amazing Pizza Place still looking for me, crying into her Coke Zero, because she missed me so much. I was going to find her, that much I knew.

We pulled up to the front of the house. 'I have one more question.'

'Shoot.' He turned off the engine.

'Do you think I'm strange?'

'Boy.' He stopped and looked at me. I could feel his eyes looking at the side of my head, even though I wasn't looking back at him. 'You are a funny kid. I'll give you that. You crack me up and you're a little weird about crowds and loud noises. Not much for talking. But you're a good kid. I think I'll keep you.'

He said 'weird,' which made me think, just for a moment, that maybe he did know my momma.

I liked Uncle Dan all right, but I had figured out over time that he had taken me from my field trip, from those bad kids that almost made me cry, from Rosalind Jane's sweaty hand. I didn't care about any of those things, but he had also taken me away from my momma. And that made me hate him. My mom wouldn't like me saying that word, but I bet she'd say it about him too if she knew that he had taken me from her. She would want me back. I just knew she wasn't dead. And I knew she would never just give me up.

We did everything together, my mom and me. We would go to coffee shops, to the grocery store, my soccer games, to Game Stop, to her work sometimes. We even went to Disney World when I was four years old with Sabrina and Christopher. I loved Disney World, except when we got to Asia, and she wouldn't let me go back and play on the dinosaurs. Then I screamed and cried until she put an ice cube on my forehead and it melted down my cheeks from the heat. Even though she was mean that one time, and made me go to bed by 8:30 pm every night, I still loved her. Since I didn't have a daddy, she did everything, picked me up from school, had my birthday parties, and made my costumes for Halloween. I knew that she was out there, waiting on me to come back, probably looking for me every day. And it had been 63 days, 6 hours, and 24 minutes since my field trip to That Amazing Pizza Place. She was probably really missing me. Every now and then I wondered if she wanted to get rid of me. I mean, maybe she gave me to Uncle Dan. I didn't think she would do that, but maybe. I just wondered why she hadn't come and gotten me if she knew that I was alive.

Uncle Dan put the truck into P. It was D for going and P for stopping. I started to memorize it in case I needed to drive somewhere some time. I unbuckled quickly and jumped out of my door.

'Not so fast, kid.' He met me at the front of the truck and put his hand on my shoulder. 'Gotta help me with these groceries.'

I looked down at his work boots and walked to the back of the truck. He handed me two bags and then he picked up the other 13 with his big hands. The veins strained in his arms, but he didn't like to make more than one trip when he shopped.

'Two trips is for losers,' he said. I wondered why he didn't use his own bags, like my momma did. Then you only had four, instead of 15 of those crinkly plastic ones.

We walked into the front door and put the groceries on the table. 'I got something to show you. I made you something while you were at school.'

I didn't care what he had made me. I knew he had lied. My momma wasn't dead. And that made me so mad. But I held my mad inside and put it into a ball, packed tight so none of it would show on my face. I took a breath and made my happy face before I looked up.

'What did you make me, Uncle Dan?'

'Oh, just your very own hideout. Come and see.'

We walked together into the back of the house, down the eleven steps of the hallway, into my bedroom. He had his hand on my shoulder the whole way. It felt like a weight sitting there, leaning my body to the left. He led me across my bedroom and opened the closet door. Then with a swish, he pushed aside the clothes, mostly ladies' clothes, that were hanging there.

'My closet?' I asked, wondering if he knew that I spent some nights sleeping in there and was mad about it.

'Look closer. Look in the back.'

There, in the far back left corner, was a little door. I didn't see it at first, because it looked just like the back wall, but it was there. I wasn't sure why, but it scared me a little. I backed away from it.

'What's in there? I'm scared. I don't want to go in there.'

'No, Pepper. It's cool. I made it just for you. It's a secret hideout. Look, you just push on this middle part, and the door pops right open.' He pushed on the door and, just like he said, it popped open. I had never seen a hidden door like that, one that looked just like the wall.

But, beyond the door, it was dark inside. I was definitely not going in there.

He reached in and pulled a switch. 'See, I even put a light in it, and some blankets, plus some snacks in case you get hungry.'

I shook my head. No way I was going in there.

'Pepper. It's for you. Here, I'll show you.'

Uncle Dan got on his hands and knees and crawled in, well, most of the way in. His legs were hanging out, but the top half of him was inside.

'See how cool it is? I made it so that it fits you. But you don't have to get in here unless you want to.'

He handed me a packet of Doritos from inside. It was the snack pack size, my favorite.

'There are other snacks in here. And some books. And look, it has this little rope so you can close the door from the inside, and you just push it when you are ready to come back out.'

He shimmied back out of the door.

'You want to give it a try?'

I didn't want to. I stood and looked at my feet. I started counting, trying to see how high I could get before he walked away. I thought he might lock me in if I went inside and never let me out. I would never see my momma if he did that.

I was on 458, when he said, 'Just stick your head in there. If you don't like it, you can come right back out.'

I didn't think it was a good idea at all.

'Come on, boy. I made this just for you. It took me all morning. Every kid needs a hideout.'

He nudged me a little, but not hard or anything. I stood, eyes on the door, and started counting again.

Then he sighed. 'Okay, Pepper. If you don't like it, then you don't have to use it. I just thought I'd do something nice for you, something to make this feel like home.'

I moved two small steps closer to the closet.

'Really, no pressure. It's there if you ever want to use it.'

I took a couple more tiny steps, like in Mother May I?

'You know, like pirates have hideouts. Now you do too. It's not like a boat or anything, but it's kind of like the tree house I had when I was a kid.'

Tree houses sounded better than a hole in the back of your closet.

'Here's the thing. If you're ever scared or feel lonely, you just crawl into your hideout and snuggle up to those blankets. I even put some juice boxes in there for you.'

I stopped at the edge of the closet. I couldn't go any closer. My legs started shaking and eyes started watering.

'Oh, Pepper. You're kind of a weird kid. Don't cry, boy. I didn't give you this to make you cry.'

He stooped down on one knee and put his arm around me.

'If you don't like it, don't use it. And if it scares you, I'll nail the thing back up again and you don't have to worry about it at all ever again.'

'Okay,' I said. I wanted him to nail it back up.

'Let's forget about it for now. Maybe you'll explore it on your own.'

I wiped my tears on my shirt. Not only would he maybe lock me in there, but there were probably monsters in the back of the tiny room behind my closet too.

He stood up and closed the closet door as I backed away. 'What do you want for dinner, kid?'

The next Saturday, Uncle Dan and I were watching football again. It was boring, but Uncle Dan kept yelling at the tv, coaching his favorite team, the Arkansas Razorbacks. I didn't really care who won, but I started counting his Pabst Blue Ribbon beers. He drank the first one, almost all in two big gulps, then burped and patted his stomach. The second and third ones were pretty quick too, as he drank them in quick sips between spicy chicken wings. I dipped my chicken nuggets into catsup and counted the empty cans as he pulled the top on number four.

'Spicy stuff,' he said and looked at me. 'You know, Pepper, you really ought to try my chicken wings. Homemade. And really, really spicy. You'd like them.'

I smiled and pretended I was more interested in the game than his beers.

'Your chicken nuggets okay?'

I nodded and put another one in my mouth so I wouldn't have to talk.

'You want anything else?'

I shook my head and kept chewing.

'Okay, then. Hand me another beer out of the ice chest. I'm getting ready to really enjoy this game.'

He drained his fourth beer while I got the fifth one. Five beers made him sleepy, but six would be better. I needed him to be really asleep.

'Hmmm,' he sighed and pulled his phone out of his pocket. 'Maybe I should call Phil and John to come over. You want to play with John outside while Phil and I watch the game?'

I froze mid-chew. I didn't want Phil and John anywhere near our house. I needed Uncle Dan to sleep.

'Y'all could take out the four runner or something.' He unlocked his phone. 'You'd like that, right?'

'Wait,' I said, trying to think of something. 'The four runner scares me. I hate the four runner.'

'What?' He put the phone down again. 'You loved it the last time I took you out on it.'

'No, it scared me. I'm afraid of turning it over accidentally and dying.' I looked up at him with my best puppy dog eyes. 'I don't want to die, Uncle Dan. Then I couldn't hang out with you every day.'

'Damn, boy. It's not that big of a deal. Don't start crying over it. You don't have to ride the four runner.'

I sniffled, trying to muster up a tear or two. I had never fake cried before, but I was willing to start today. 'It's just,' I started. 'It's just that I want to watch the game by ourselves today. I'm really having fun, aren't you?'

His face cracked into a smile. 'Yeah, I'm having fun too, Pepper. Hell, the first quarter's over anyway, so they probably don't want to come over in the middle of the game no how.'

He patted me on the head, and I made myself not shrink from his touch.

'Scared of the four runner, who would've thought. You are a funny kid, you know that?'

I smiled and nodded and we went back to the game.

Number five went pretty slowly. He was starting to get up every ten minutes to pee out the back door. The screen door would slam behind him, loud, too loud. It hurt my ears every time. And then I would hear him peeing. I wasn't sure why he peed outside when he drank beer. Finally, he opened number six. I knew number six would be the magic number. He drank about half of it, then settled back on the couch. I sat on the floor, the coffee table chest high, and put all of the leftovers back into the box. I had kept my shoes on the whole time, ready to creep outside as soon as I could. I watched his eyes take long blinks before he leaned his head onto the back of the couch. They fluttered closed and his hand relaxed around the remote. He started breathing slow and heavy, not quite snoring. I counted to 6,048 by twos before I moved a muscle. Then I slowly got my feet underneath me. I stood up, my left knee popping. Uncle Dan didn't move, though, just snorted a little, then kept breathing heavily through his open mouth. I crept closer to him, keeping my feet silent, ninja style. I reached for the phone, which lay on his lap. His hand jumped, scaring me to death, but I didn't scream or run. I just stood there, paralyzed, leaning over his lap, holding his phone.

Don't wake up. Don't wake up. Don't wake up. Don't wake up. I saw the words in my brain over and over. Three words that kept him asleep as long as I said them silently in my brain. I wanted to yell them out, 'Don't wake up!' But I knew that if I did, then I would never get to make that phone call.

My hands were sweating, but I kept a tight hold anyway. I had to get outside, where I could breathe, and make this phone call. I tiptoed toward the back door, toward the chickens. I would be careful to stay quiet. They were sleeping and I didn't want to get them squawking so that they woke Uncle Dan up.

I made it to the back door and turned the knob slowly. It was pretty quiet, but I knew that door creaked when it opened, so I was slow to pull it back. An inch at a time, I eased it open. It squeaked some, but mostly I made myself count to 30 for every inch, so it didn't make too much noise. I could see the back of Uncle Dan's head over the edge of the couch. He was still heavy breathing, and now making snoring noises. This was my chance, and I didn't want to lose it.

I made it through the back door, then out the screen door, holding it so that it wouldn't slam behind me. I was a ninja, sneaky and small, so quiet that no one would notice that I was gone. I steadied my hands and made myself go slowly so that the boards on the back porch didn't creak.

I made it outside, counting and holding my breath until I was dizzy. It felt like if I didn't breathe, then maybe, just maybe, he wouldn't hear me and would stay asleep. I stepped into the cool night air, looking up at the stars one more time. I had never counted them all before. I had tried, but there were too many. I wanted to count them now, but I knew I had to call my momma before it was too late.

I got the paper out of my pocket. Hank had come into my classroom to bring some papers to Ms. D. He slipped the paper on my desk, all folded into a little ball. I put my hand over it straight away, but let it sit there until he left the room. Then I pocketed it. When I unfolded it later, during recess, I saw three magic numbers, 901. Like Morse code, I was sure these numbers would find my momma.

I dialed my number, each button beeping as I pressed it. I put 901 at the end of the number and got the same lady on the recording. 'Beep, beep, beep. I'm sorry, but your call cannot be connected at this time. Please check the number and try again.' I tried it again: 373-1888-901. I couldn't believe that Hank had given me the wrong number.

I looked up at the stars and counted to 157. I had to focus. I knew he told me that these numbers had to go with the other seven of my momma's. I thought back to his face, his mouth moving with the words. 'Try putting three numbers in front there.'

'In front!' I had put them behind my numbers. I always got in front and behind confused. I tried again. I knew I didn't have much time. 901-373-1888.

It rang six times before it went to her voicemail. But there it was, her voice. I knew it was her voice from the first word, 'Hi, you've reached Katherine Armsteaden. I'm not available at the moment, but, if you leave a message, I'll be sure to call you back.'

I got so excited that I started jumping up and down. There it was. Her voice. She was alive! I knew he had lied. My momma wasn't in heaven. I hung up at the end of the message. I couldn't believe it was her voice. She was right there in the phone. I knew she must be alive, but why didn't she answer?

I called the numbers again, and it went to her voicemail again after six rings. I loved hearing her name: 'Katherine Armsteaden.' I had almost forgotten it, not her face or her numbers, but her name. Just for a minute, it had slipped away from my mind, but her voice reminded me of how much I missed her.

'Momma,' I said. 'It's Pepper. I'm here. I'm alive. I miss you. You have to come and get me.' I panicked for a second. I hadn't thought this through. I didn't even know what city I lived in. 'Don't call me back. Uncle Dan will know that I tried to call you if you call me back.' I tried to catch my breath. My heart was beating so fast and so hard in my chest that I had to keep my legs from jumping, jumping. 'I'm here, Momma. And I'm going to call you back and tell you where I am, so you can come and get me. Please come and get me.' I thought for a second. 'I love you. Don't call me back. Or... or he might kill me. Please don't call me back.'

I hung up the phone and deleted the call. If she didn't call back, then Uncle Dan would never know. Oh, I hoped she was okay and would listen to her messages.

I leaned over into the grass and threw up the chicken nuggets and Dr Pepper that I had had for dinner. I wasn't sure why, but I had never thrown up without my momma there, and it scared me a little and my eyes leaked a few tears. Please, please, let her hear my message. Please let her come and get me. How could she come and get me? I didn't even tell her what town I was in. I didn't even know what town I was in.

I wiped my mouth on my sleeve and looked over at the chickens. They were all in their coop, making eggs for our breakfast. I sure hoped my momma would get here before then. I tiptoed back into the house, careful not to creak the door. I put the phone in Uncle Dan's hand, which made him wake up.

'What? What you need, boy?' he asked, squinting his eyes at me, like he was looking at the sun.

'Nothing,' I said. 'Can I play on your phone? It's half time.'

He roused. 'What's the score?'

I froze and looked at the tv. I wasn't even sure who the two teams were, and I definitely didn't know the score.

'Uh, I'm not sure. I don't think I have the hang of football yet.'

'Look, boy,' he sat up and looked at the tv. 'Football is an American pastime. You're going to see a lot of it around here, so you need to know what's going on.' He paused and looked at me. 'Grab me a beer out of the cooler and I'll teach you all about scoring and stats. You love numbers. You're going to love stats.'

I got him the beer and handed it to him. He popped it open with one hand and sipped the first half before he started explaining what stats were. I pretended to be interested and nodded my head, asking appropriate 'confused' questions. 'So, what's third down mean?' 'When do they kick a field goal?' 'What does offsides mean?' I already knew most of it, but wanted to keep Uncle Dan talking so that I could watch his phone in case my momma called back.

But she didn't. I waited all that night and the next day. She didn't call me back. She didn't come and get me. I couldn't figure it out. Why wouldn't she come and get me? I lay in bed all night, thinking about my momma, trying to figure out what I did wrong. I had called her. I knew she could see the number on her phone. Couldn't she find out where I was with the number? Wasn't there some sort of

151

GPS thing with cell phones, so you could track them or something? I knew I should have figured out the name of the town so I could tell her. That could make it a ton easier for her. I knew she would come eventually. I just had to give her more time.

Sunday went a lot like Saturday, only with less beer. Uncle Dan had drunk all of the beer on Saturday, and we lived 'in a dry county, at least on Sundays' he said, so he couldn't get more until Monday. He watched football for most of the day, explaining to me the positions: the quarterback, the safety, the fullback.

I pretended to watch football and nodded when he talked to me. I even looked him in the eyes, so he would think that I really understood what he was saying. But mostly I watched his phone and the front drive. I would spend 15 minutes watching his phone, waiting for it to light up, for a text to come in, something from my momma. I didn't know what I would do if she really did text back and he saw it, but I hoped he would nap or get drunk, or something, and I could grab it quick from his hand before he noticed. Then I would tell Uncle Dan that I had to pee or needed a Dr Pepper or snack, and I would walk toward the kitchen, looking out the back window. I just knew I would see her gray Ford Freestyle pulling up in the driveway. But, every time I went by, nobody was there, just the chickens that had figured out how to fly out of their coop.

Come on, Momma, I thought. You have to come and get me. I left you a message.

By Sunday night, I thought my momma was dead after all. If not, she would have come and gotten me. I cried that night, lying in the bed, feeling my tears roll down into my ears. I had figured out her number. Now she had to come and get me. Where was she? Why wasn't she here, picking me up? I felt so stupid not remembering the town. But nobody ever told me what town it was. How was I supposed to know? I counted the lines in the ceiling by the moonlight, even though I already knew there were 387. Somehow it calmed me down, though. I wondered if she could see the same moon that I saw. I thought about the hole in the back of my closet. Maybe if I slept in there then Uncle Dan would forget about me. But it was night time and I was too scared to get out of bed. I was way too scared to get into that creepy hole. I fell asleep on the fifth time counting the boards on the ceiling.

On Monday, Uncle Dan woke me up as the sun was coming up. I stared out at the driveway. No sign of my momma. He gave me pancakes and bacon, two of my favorites. I just looked at them, sick to my stomach again.

'Come on, boy,' he said when he realized I wasn't eating. 'You want to be big and strong like your Uncle Dan, don't you?'

I looked at him with the meanest eyes I could think of. He wasn't my Uncle Dan. Even though he had the gold tooth, he wasn't my uncle at all.

'Pepper. Don't look at me that way, or I'll skin you alive.' He paused. 'What's wrong with you, boy? Didn't we have a fun weekend?'

I made my mean eyes look away. I didn't want him to know what I had done. I nodded.

'I don't even know what your nods mean, kid. What's going on with you?'

I looked at him, shoveling runny yellow eggs into his mouth and talking at the same time. No one related to my momma would have manners to talk with his mouth full. I shrugged.

'No shrugging. Tell me what's wrong.' He held onto my arm and got his face close to mine. 'Talk to me, Pepper.'

I counted his whiskers again, fast, getting up to 589 before I answered him. 'Nothing. Nothing's wrong.'

He didn't believe me and kept his face right next to my nose.

'Seriously. Tell me, Pepper. I can help.'

I shrugged again and kept counting: The six hundreds went quickly. What could I tell him?

'Okay,' he backed up and took in another mouthful of eggs. 'If you don't tell me what's wrong, then no more Angry Birds.'

I felt a wailing in my chest. My heart started beating and it felt like somebody was sitting on top of it. I couldn't see his whiskers anymore, but my heart was pounding out numbers inside of me. He couldn't do that. He couldn't take away my Angry Birds. I started to cry, and had to say something.

'It's just...' I started. I couldn't think of anything to say. 'It's just that the smell of eggs makes me want to barf.'

His face cracked into a too-wide smile again. 'Pepper, all you gotta do is tell me. I can go over here by the sink and eat these eggs if it bothers you that much.' He picked up his plate and stood over the sink. 'I just want you happy, kid.'

He dropped me off at school that day, and I was both relieved to get away from him and hopeful I would be able to call my momma again. But what if she called his phone while I was gone? And then she couldn't get me because he would be so mad that he would hit me again? What if he came to school and got me out of class because he was so mad? What if she couldn't find me? All of these thoughts flooded in and out of my head, like a wave crashing onto the beach with no relief.

It was hard to wait, and I kept trying to pay attention during circle time, but all anyone wanted to do was talk about what they did over the weekend. I kept my mouth shut and listened to the clock tick, counting the seconds in each minute that passed. We finally went back to our desks and started math. It was so easy. I finished mine in ten minutes, but I waited until 10:07, watching the hands on the clock, until I knew Ms. Harrison would be ready to take a break. I knew we didn't have anything until 10:35, when we had to go to music.

'I'm done,' I said to Ms. Harrison. 'I feel so sleepy. Can we walk the stairs?'

'Sleepy?' she asked. 'Since when are you sleepy?'

I put my hands on my head. 'My head is about to explode. My brain is all turned upside down today. Can we go walk the stairs?'

She sighed. 'Okay. Hang on.'

She walked over to Ms. D.'s desk as I watched the seconds tick off the clock. It was 10:08. I had to get out of there and on her phone.

'Ms. Drozinsky, is it okay if Pepper and I go walk the stairs? He's feeling kind of antsy and he finished his math work.'

Ms. Drozinsky nodded and I almost ran to the door. I headed for the stairs and the teachers' lounge. We went up the stairs, then back down, then all of the way up. I was taking them two at a time, trying to get Ms. Harrison to hurry.

'Slow down, Pepper. I have to go to the bathroom.' We walked down the hall to the teachers' lounge. 'Stay here for a second. I'll be right back.' She started walking away.

'Wait,' I said. 'Can I play on your phone? Can I play Angry Birds?'

'Just wait. I'll only be a second, not even long enough to play Angry Birds.'

My legs started jumping as she said that. 'Please, please. I never get to play at home. Uncle Dan won't let me.'

She stopped for a second. 'Uncle Dan? What?' Then she shook it off, and said, 'Okay, here. But I'm only going to be a minute. Do not leave this spot, this exact spot on the floor. Don't leave it, and I mean it.'

I smiled up at her. 'I won't. Pinky swear.' I held out my pinky and she laughed with her white, white teeth as she wrapped her finger around mine.

I dialed my momma's numbers as she walked away. She picked up on the second ring.

'Pepper?' she said. 'Pepper, is this you?'

At first I couldn't even speak. I opened my mouth and the words didn't come out. It was her. It was my momma. After all this time, she was alive. She was there, and now I couldn't even make my brain push the words out of my mouth. I sat down on the ground for a second and counted to ten really fast like she always told me to. Then I took a deep breath. I had to talk to her. This might be my only chance.

'Come on, Pepper. If this is you, you have to talk to me. Take a deep, even breath in and let it out. Then tell me where you are.'

I took another breath in.

'Momma! You're alive! You're alive.' I whispered, but walked fast down the hall, away from the teachers' lounge, so Ms. Harrison wouldn't hear me. My tennis shoes squeaked on the blue tiles under each foot. I was careful to only step on the blue ones as I made my way toward the end of the hall.

'Of course I am, Pepper. And you're alive! I got your message, but the phone number didn't show up on my phone. It just said restricted. I've been going nuts trying to find you, Pepper. I've gone to the police. Everybody is looking for you. Where are you, honey?'

'I don't know. Where are you?'

'I'm in Memphis, Pepper. You have to tell me where you are so that the police and I can find you.'

'You're not in heaven? I thought you were in heaven.'

'No, Pepper. I'm in Memphis. I thought you were in heaven. I couldn't find you and I've been looking and looking for you.'

'I don't have much time, Momma. Ms. Harrison just went to the bathroom for a minute. You can't call me back, because then she'll know I'm not playing Angry Birds. You have to come and get me, Momma.' I started to cry, hearing her voice and wondering where she was. I was nearing the end of the hall.

'Take a deep breath, Pepper, and count to ten. I'm going to come and get you, honey. Me and the police. But I have to find you. We tried to trace that number you called from before…'

'Uncle Dan's phone? Don't call him back either.'

'I didn't, honey. I couldn't. It said restricted and the police couldn't either. What city, Pepper? You have to tell me.'

'I don't know where I am. I don't know the city.' I hadn't been able to find out the city name yet. 'I only know that I found 901 so that I could call you.'

'Baby, you have to tell me where you are. What do you see?'

I could see Ms. Harrison walking down the hall toward me. I started walking away from her. First I went up the stairs, then out the side door toward the playground. I had to talk to my momma for a minute.

'I saw Ms. Harrison and she's coming my way, so I ran up the stairs and out the door to the playground. Ms. Harrison is coming for me, though. Even though I can run really fast, I have to go.'

'Do not hang up, Pepper,' Momma said in her I-mean-business voice, like when she wanted me to buckle my seatbelt in the car or clean up my toys before bedtime. 'Who's Ms. Harrison?' She was talking fast.

'She's kind of my teacher and kind of my friend. I'm running away from her and she's going to be so mad.' I looked back and saw her running toward me, getting closer with each step.

'Pepper, are you at school? Give the phone to Ms. Harrison. I want to talk to her. She can help us. Is she someone who would help you?'

'Yes, I'm at school. And I don't know. Don't ask me so many questions, Momma. You're making my head spinny.' I ran toward the slides and climbed to the very top of the ladder, 1, 2, 3, 4, 5, 6, 7, 8, 9, 10, up the stairs, all of the way into the tunnel that ran between the two slides. I could hear her steps on the ladder. Her own feet did their own 1, 2, 3, 4, 5, but then they stopped. I wondered if she was going to go back down the steps. I kept listening for 5, 4, 3, 2, 1, but there was nothing.

'Honey, you have to tell me. What's the name of your school? Do you know the name of your school? Then I can come and find you.'

I was out of breath. I couldn't remember the name of the school and my momma needed it. 'I'm not sure. I can't remember.'

'Pepper? Are you in the tunnel?' Ms. Harrison was yelling at me, but kind of quiet, like she didn't want anyone to hear.

I didn't answer, but Momma kept talking.

'Yes, you can, baby. It's easy. Just see the words in your head. You can even see the letters and spell it out if that's easier.'

She was breathing heavily, like she had been running too. 'I'm trying, Momma. It starts with an 'O.' O-S-C-A-R...'

I saw Ms. Harrison's hands reach the top of the ladder. I could hear her voice clearer now.

'Pepper, you're in so much trouble. You better come down here right now.' 6, 7, 8, 9, 10. I wanted enough time to add up all of her steps and divide them by 20 to see what it came out to, but there was no time left. No hours, no minutes, no seconds. She was crawling into the tunnel with me.

I looked at the phone one last time before hanging up. 'Come and get me, Momma. I have to go. I love you.'

I felt Ms. Harrison grab my arm, knocking the phone out of my hands onto the plastic slide. I watched it slide toward the bottom and I didn't have a chance to delete my mom's number.

'Pepper Johnson. You're never going to use my phone again. What were you doing? Who were you calling, China?'

She laughed, but I knew she was angry. I felt my heart pounding in my chest. For a second, I thought it might fall out of my chest. I had found my mom. Now she could come and get me. I talked to her. She wasn't dead. I knew she wasn't dead all along. Ms. Harrison started whisper yelling again.

'Look at me.' She pulled my chin toward her eyes. 'In the face. You can never, ever run away from me again. Understand? I mean never. You might have gotten hurt or run over by a car or something. And then you would be dead, and I would get fired and in so much trouble, it wouldn't even be funny.'

She paused as I was trying to catch my breath. 'Are you listening to me?' I wasn't, but I nodded my head anyway.

She caught my chin in her pointer finger again. 'You better look at me, Pepper, because I'm serious.' I looked at her eyes. They were the darkest eyes I had ever seen, but not mean, even though she was mad. She pulled me out of the tunnel and down the ladder.

'Tell me that you'll never run out of school or away from me again. Tell me that right now.'

'Okay.' I looked down at my shoes on the grass.

'No,' she said with her mean voice. 'You look at me and say, "I will never run out of school or away from you again, Ms. Harrison."'

'Okay, okay. I'm sorry. My brain got all mixed up and I just wanted to play on your phone, but I promise that I'll never run away from you again.' I wondered if I could tell her that I was talking to my momma. I didn't know if I could trust her or if she would tell Uncle Dan, who would be so mad that he might hit me again.

'Well, you're grounded from my phone. That's for sure. So you can just get over that.'

I looked down. 'I'm sorry. I'm so sorry. So, so sorry. I didn't mean to. Please don't be mad. I hate it when you're mad at me.' I started crying a little.

Ms. Harrison pulled me toward the bottom of the slide and grabbed her phone. She looked it over and shoved it in her back pocket. She grabbed my hand and started walking fast toward the school. She wasn't being nice at all. I kept listening for her phone to ring. I was sure my momma would call right back.

The whole way back Ms. Harrison fussed at me. 'I can't believe you would do this to me. I thought we were friends. I thought I could trust you.'

She kept walking fast, almost running, toward the school. I walked as slowly as I could, dragging my feet along the dust. She pulled at my arm, trying to get me to go faster. I felt the tears run down my face, getting my shirt all wet.

'You could have gotten me fired, Pepper. You're not even supposed to use my phone. I just let you do that when you act good and finish up all of your work. But no more of that. You've ruined that.'

I stopped and sat down on the ground. I couldn't stand Ms. Harrison being mad at me. She was the only friend I had. I cried into my shirt, lifting the front of it over my eyes so she wouldn't see me. 'I'm sorry. I'm sorry.' The tears came out and I couldn't stop them. 'I just wanted to see my momma. I miss her so much.'

There, I had said it. I had told her about my momma. I wiped my nose on my sleeve.

She stopped walking and stooped down next to me. 'Shit, Pepper.'

I couldn't believe she cussed. It scared me so bad that I stopped crying for a second and looked up at her.

'Not shit. Shoot. Don't tell anyone that I cussed. I know you miss your momma. I can't even imagine. It must be hard for a little boy. Heck, it would be hard for anyone. I would hate it if I couldn't be with my mom.'

I thought for a second that she might start crying too. Maybe she couldn't find her momma either.

'Did you lose your momma too?' I asked her.

'No, Pepper. I still have my momma. I'm super lucky. But you'll see your momma one day.

Just wait and see. And, in the meantime, you just remember that she's watching over you all the time.' She hesitated for a second and tucked her hair behind her ear. 'You want to make your momma proud, don't you?'

I nodded and wiped snot on the inside of my shirt.

'Well, then, no more running away from me. You nearly scared me to death, boy. I thought you weren't coming back.' She put her hand on my arm. 'Your momma wouldn't want you to run away. She would want you to do your best in school, to finish your work, and to be happy.'

'Okay,' I sniffled.

'Can you try that for me?'

I nodded.

'And for your momma?'

I nodded again.

'Now, let's go get you cleaned up. You can't walk around school with tears and snot streaming down your face.'

'Okay.'

'And, Pepper, I'm sorry I got mad at you. I was just scared.'

When she said it, I stopped for a second. I never knew that people got mad when they got scared. I just got scared. But maybe that's why Uncle Dan got mad at me sometimes, or seemed like it. Maybe he was scared. I wasn't sure that anything could scare him, not being bitten by a fish or cutting the heads off our chickens. But maybe he was scared of getting caught.

I stayed close to Ms. Harrison for the rest of the day, thinking that Momma would call her back, call me back, and Ms. Harrison could tell her the city we were in. Her phone didn't ring, but maybe she put it on silent. I wasn't sure. She wouldn't let me even look at it anymore. She kept it in her pocket the whole time.

I kept as quiet as I could, just waiting to hear it ring or at least vibrate. Right before I left for the carpool line, I tugged on her shirt and looked at her in the eye, like my momma told me to do when I wanted to make sure someone was listening to me. 'I'm sorry about today, Ms. Harrison. I really am.'

'I know, Pepper. It's okay. We all have bad days every now and then. Tomorrow will be better, right? Can you promise me that tomorrow will be better?'

I kept looking her in the eyes, even though it made my brain hurt. I nodded. 'Yes, I promise.'

'Good. That's my boy. You'll be fine by morning. Now go on and get into the carpool line.'

'Okay, but Ms. Harrison?'

'Yeah, Pepper. What do you need?'

'What city are we in?'

She laughed. 'You ask me the craziest questions, kid. What are you talking about, Pepper?'

'The city. What city is this?'

'Well, it's not really a city. It's more like a town, a small town.' Then she added under her breath, but I heard her, 'One that I really need to get the heck out of.'

'What is the name of it, though?'

'Pepper. These are all things you should already know. Your phone number, your address. You know this stuff already, right? I mean, don't you?'

'I just forgot the city's name. Sometimes I lose words. Like they are sitting in the front of my brain, but I can't get them to my mouth. Does that ever happen to you?' My palms started to sweat, because I didn't think she was going to tell me.

She sighed. 'Yeah. Sometimes. But then it comes to me at the weirdest times, like when I'm trying to sleep.' She looked at me and slowed down her talking. 'Arthursville, Pepper. Arthursville, that's our town. And tomorrow we can discuss the difference between a city and a town. You need to know this stuff. For social studies. And your own safety. You have to know how to get home if you ever get lost, you know.'

I kept thinking, I know. I know. That's why I need to know the city name, so I can get home. But I pretended like I had just forgotten. 'Can you spell it so that I can remember? I need to remember it.'

'Sure, Pepper. It's A-R-T-H-U-R-S-V-I-L-L-E. I know, it's kind of long, but you can remember that now, right?'

I closed my eyes and saw the letters. I saw them in my head and tried to burn them in there so I wouldn't forget. It was really long, longer than Memphis. And it had taken me four years to remember Memphis. But I tried to imprint the letters on my brain, to burn them there so I wouldn't forget. Quickly, I transferred the letters into numbers. Like Ms. Drozinsky's name. 1-18-20-8-21-18-19-22-9-12-12-5. There, I had it. I had to tell my mom where I was. I had to help her find me.

Uncle Dan drove up, so I was about to leave. 'And the state? What's the state?'

'Pepper, come on. We already did this in social studies. You really don't remember?'

'It starts with an "A", right?'

'Yes. And it's not Alaska or Alabama. Any ideas?'

Uncle Dan tooted the horn on his truck and waved at me to get in the car.

'Go now. There's your dad.'

'Wait. Tell me. What's the state? It's important. Like you said.'

She pushed me toward Uncle Dan's truck. 'Ar-kansas, Pepper. Arkansas is our state. Arthursville is our town. And tomorrow we brush up on our social studies.'

I nodded and walked toward the truck. She didn't follow me, which I thought she might, because I thought she would tell him about me acting bad that day. Luckily, Uncle Dan had the windows rolled up, so he didn't hear what she said to me.

Ms. Harrison let me go, and didn't say one word to him about me running away. I guess she really had forgiven me. He drove us to the Sonic and bought me a chocolate milkshake and some chicken nuggets and french fries. They were my favorites, but I knew the truth now, and I could barely even swallow the milkshake without wanting to barf again. He had one of their 17 styles of hot dogs, the kind with chili, cheese, sauerkraut, ketchup, mustard, and pickles. I loved hot dogs, but never told him, because I was afraid he would try to make me eat all of that other stuff that he put on his hot dog. I didn't even know how you could taste the hot dog with all of that stuff on it. I liked my hot dogs like I liked my hamburgers, meat and cheese, nothing else to mess it up.

He kept trying to talk to me. 'How was your day, boy?'

I shrugged. I didn't care what he bought me. He had lied to me and wasn't my uncle.

'You have any tests today?'

I didn't look at him, only shrugged again.

'Come on, kid. What's wrong with you? Something happen at school?'

I shook my head no and stirred my milkshake with my straw.

'Pepper. You know how mad it makes me when you just shrug your shoulders and don't talk. You gotta talk to me. What happened?'

I didn't want to make him mad. I was going to help my momma find me no matter what. I reviewed the letters of this city in my head over and over. I saw them there, hanging like shirts on a clothesline. I would spell it for her when I called her again. I wasn't sure how I would do that, but maybe Uncle Dan would drink his six beers again and fall asleep. It was only a matter of time, I told myself. This time, I would tell my momma exactly where I was.

He snapped his fingers in front of my face. 'Pepper? Earth to Pepper? Why are you spacing out, kid?'

I still didn't look at him, but answered, 'Sorry. Today was fine. I'm really tired. Can I take a nap when we get home?'

'After homework you can. Gotta do the time, Pepper. Gotta work hard to get the things you want.'

I swished some chocolate milkshake around in my mouth. I didn't know what 'do the time' meant, but I had been waiting forever to talk to my momma. I had to figure out a way.

'You liking those chicken nuggets and french fries? Because you're hardly eating any of them. You know how I feel about wasted food.'

I knew we could just give them to the chickens. They loved french fries, and even chicken nuggets, which I found kind of weird because it was like they were eating their long lost cousins or something.

I dipped a chicken nugget into some ketchup and shoved it in my mouth. It tasted like cardboard, but I chewed it so he wouldn't get mad. I didn't want to act weird at all. I didn't want him to suspect anything.

'They are good,' I said, and smiled at him, so he would think that I liked him.

'Good. I know it's early, but this is dinner for tonight. I don't feel like cooking and it's Monday night, football tonight.'

I nodded. Maybe that meant he would drink a lot and I could use his phone.

'You can have a snack later if you want one, but I thought we would get an early supper and get that out of the way.'

He shoved the last of his hot dog into his mouth and started the engine.

I counted the lines on the road again until we got home. I tried to keep quiet, but answered his questions when he asked me them.

He didn't drink any beer that night, and put me to bed at 8:30 pm. Still my momma didn't come for me. I didn't understand why she didn't come. Maybe she couldn't find me. She needed to know what city. Again, I counted the boards in the ceiling, then my heartbeats. Then I just counted on my fingers, over and over, touching each one with my thumb as I got up to 4,587. I didn't think I would ever fall asleep. I didn't have a clock, but I figured it was after midnight before I fell asleep, and even then I had dreams where I kept running away from a big monster that was trying to get me.

I jolted awake when I heard the yelling. There were big, mean man voices, louder even than Uncle Dan. They were screaming and beating on the door. I jumped out of my bed and saw bright lights outside. The whole yard and the chicken coop were all lit up, and I couldn't see past the lights, but the voices kept screaming, telling me to 'Get down. Hands up. Open the door.' I dropped to the floor, held up my hands (just in case they could see me), and crawled toward my closet. I had to hide. And, as scared as I was of the hole in the back of my closet, I was even more scared of the men yelling at the door. It was like a war and they were attacking us. I only had a few seconds.

I had to hide from them. I had to get back to my momma. Play the game, I told myself, The Survival Game. Survive, I ordered myself and ran for the closet.

The front door broke open with a bang just as I closed the closet door. I didn't want to open the scary hole door in the back, but I was afraid they would get me if I didn't. I had to get back to my momma, so I couldn't let anyone else get me. Just when I was so close, some men had come to try to take me. Right when I was about to tell my momma the city I was in so that I could go home.

I heard Uncle Dan yelling as I scrambled into the hole and closed the door behind me. It was dark in there. Pitch black. And it was kind of hot. I guess you had to leave the door open for the cool air to come in, but I wasn't about to do that, or the mean men would get me. And no telling how they might be. They might take me to some other city, and then I would have to figure that out so that I could tell my momma. They might hurt me and never let me see my momma again.

I felt around for the flashlight that Uncle Dan had said he had left for me. I didn't want to turn on the big light. I was afraid they would see it under the door. I felt three juice boxes and some packets of what turned out to be Doritos before I found the flashlight. I turned it on and looked around. Besides a blanket and the snacks, there wasn't much else in there. I wondered how much oxygen I had in this hole. I hoped it wouldn't run out before the bad men left. I heard them stomping through the house, yelling at Uncle Dan, who just kept saying, 'I'm the only one here. There's no one else.' Every now and then, he would say really loudly, 'Who? I don't know what you're talking about.'

I could hear them running from room to room, yelling out, 'Clear.' I turned out the flashlight so that they wouldn't know where I was. They couldn't find me. No matter what. I had my survival plan. They had to leave me there so that my momma could come and get me. They even opened up the closet door, but they didn't find the hole door, because it looked just like the back of the closet unless you moved the hanging clothes out of the way and looked really close. They were in my room, opening my drawers, pulling things out from under my bed, lifting up the mattress and looking under it. I heard it all from the hole. I covered my ears to try to make the sound quieter. They were so loud and I didn't like people yelling at all. People talked way too much and they yelled way, way too much. I slowed down my breathing and stayed quiet, being careful so that they wouldn't find me. I kept sweating in there, trying not to breathe too deep, hoping to conserve the air in the closet hole. I did the even breathing that my momma taught me. First, 1, 2, 3, 4, 5 in. Then, 1, 2, 3, 4, 5 out. It calmed me a little bit and made me feel like the air would hold out until the bad men left. I held in my tears, but I wanted to cry out for my momma. I didn't know why things were so messed up. I was just about to get home to her when those stupid mean men broke down Uncle Dan's door and started tearing up the house. I wondered if they looked in the chicken coop. I bet they scared the chickens with all of their yelling. They probably wouldn't lay any eggs for days.

I listened and waited for what seemed like hours, until the last of their feet left the house. I thought that maybe I could come out soon. I opened a juice box, thinking it might make me stop sweating. I didn't really like to sweat. It was dripping down my back and making me all itchy. And my throat was dry so I slowly opened up the crinkly plastic and stuck the straw into the box. The sweetness filled my mouth and I felt much better, like the fist in my throat was opening up a little bit. I breathed in and out, as quietly as I could, counting with each breath: 1, 2, 3, 4, 5, 6, 7 in. 1, 2, 3, 4, 5, 6, 7 out. I had watched my momma do that, 'even breathing,' she had called it, making the breathing in breath the same as the breathing out breath. It made my heart not beat so fast when I did it. Soon they would be gone and I could get back to my momma. I waited. I was good at waiting. I could wait a really long time if I needed to. There was no way I was going to let the mean men get me.

It got quiet after a while, but the lights were still there. At least they weren't yelling or stomping through the house anymore. One by one, they started to turn off and I could hear the cars start to drive away. I didn't hear Uncle Dan anymore, which scared me a little bit. I didn't want to sleep in this house, in this hole, all night by myself. What if they took him away and left me all alone? Maybe they left his phone and I could call my momma and tell her the name of the town. I had it in my brain this time: Arthursville.

I was thinking all of this through when I heard it. It was soft at first, like it was muffled by a cry or something, but I knew who it was the minute I heard it.

'Pepper.'

Her voice seemed to choke on my name and I hesitated until she cried out again. 'Pepper. Oh, my sweet boy.'

It was my momma. Right there in the front yard of Uncle Dan's house. And she was leaving. She was leaving with the mean men who had torn up Uncle Dan's house. Oh no. I could hear them driving away. She had come to get me and I almost missed her. My heart jumped and I couldn't believe that she had come all this way and she was going to leave without me.

'Momma!' I yelled, but I'm sure she didn't hear me inside of the closet hole. 'Momma, wait!' Hurry, hurry. Hands and knees. Get out now. Crawl toward the door. Push on the door so you can get out. Stay low and keep your hands in the air so they won't shoot you. Move, Pepper, I ordered myself. Survive and get back to Momma.

I scrambled out of the hole door, juice box still in my hand. I couldn't think. I couldn't do anything but go to her voice. It had been so long. I couldn't lose her now. 'Momma.'

I didn't hear anything as I pushed open the closet door and saw the mess in my room. Uncle Dan was going to be so mad. His fist would ball up and the vein in his neck would pulse with his heartbeat. I knew I should stop and clean it up. I picked up a pair of my jeans and put them on the bed. Clothes were everywhere. My mattress was ripped up and the stuffing was falling all over the floor. I thought I could probably clean it up really quick, but then I heard her again. I leaned down and picked up a handful of the stuffing and put it back into the slit in the mattress. It was going to take me a while to clean it all up, but at least Uncle Dan wouldn't be so mad if I got started.

'He has to be in there. Just let me look.' Then louder this time, 'Pepper!'

'Momma.'

Then I threw down the juice box and left everything a mess in my room. I didn't care what Uncle Dan did. I had to get to my momma. She was right outside. I could hear her voice. And she was saying my name. I stopped for a second. Was it a trap set by the mean men? What if they recorded her voice and played it outside of the house to try to capture me? Why would they want to capture me? Why would anyone want to take me? I couldn't figure it out, but I had to get out there and look either way.

Run, feet, run. She's right there. Get to her, fast. I ran out of my room and down the hall into the kitchen, counting my steps, 1, 2, 3. 1, 2, 3. 1, 2, 3. I kept getting stuck on three, and I wasn't sure why. I had never been stuck on a number before, but there I was, stuck on three and unable to go any further. But I figured that I could do 1, 2, 3 over and over until I got out the front door. I just kept telling my feet to keep moving. I stopped when I entered the kitchen. Oh no, oh no. Uncle Dan was going to be furious. I had to make sure not to get near his fists when he saw the kitchen. It was an even bigger mess than my room. They had taken all of the food out of the refrigerator and thrown it on the floor. The cabinets were open and everything in them was spilling out, over the countertops, on the floor. The chairs and tables were turned over. The whole place was a mess.

I stopped for a second to take it all in, then looked at my feet again. It was like they didn't know how to move all of a sudden. Run, feet. You have to run. I took off in a sprint across the room. I slid across spilled milk and sweet relish as I was running for the door. My socks soaked up the milk, which felt weird between my toes, but I kept going until I reached the front door.

I turned the handle and felt relieved that it was unlocked. I guessed the mean men had left it unlocked. I swung the door open and nearly ran into the screen door. I heard it slam behind me, like a gunshot ringing out into the night air. It was loud and I wanted to cover my ears, but I had to get to her. 1, 2, 3. 1, 2, 3. Just a few more 1, 2, 3s and I would be near her voice. I would feel her soft hair and her cheek against mine. I would smell her vanilla and know that I was home again. I stopped right outside the front door. There were still a few bright lights shining in my eyes so I couldn't see much of anything, just the outline of some of the cars.

I yelled again, 'Momma,' as loud as I could. Maybe she would hear me. Maybe she stayed long enough to hear me. Please don't let her have gone away. I can't have lost her twice. Please don't let this be a trap that the mean men have set. I have to get back to my momma. I looked over at the chicken coop, but didn't see any chickens. I wondered if the mean men had let them out of their fence. Uncle Dan was going to be hopping mad about all sorts of things.

'There he is. Oh God, there he is.' I heard her say, then she yelled to me, 'Pepper, stay right there! Honey, I'm coming.'

It was her! It was really her! I could hear her and she was talking to me. I started running toward her voice, but the men with the mean voices stopped me on 1, 2 and told me to stay where I was. One of them yelled, 'Freeze. Do not move.'

I didn't understand why they didn't want me to move. I had to move. I had to get to my momma. I knew what 'freeze' meant. I had played Freeze Tag and knew how to act like a statue. I stopped and looked down at my socks, which were muddy as the dirt mixed with the milk. There was some relish smeared on the top of my left sock. I started counting the green specks to try to make the time go faster until I was with my mom. She was right there. I knew she was. I couldn't see her, but I could hear her, and, unless these men were playing a trick on me, then I was closer than ever to my momma. I wanted to take my socks off, but I froze and was scared to take another step.

'For God's sake. That's him. That's Pepper! I told you he was in there.' I heard my momma tell the men.

Then to me she said, 'Baby, don't move. I'll come and get you.'

'Where are you, Momma?' I could hear her voice just fine, but had to squint into the bright lights. 'My socks have milk and relish all over them.'

'Pepper, stay where you are. We just want to check you over real quick. Then you can see your mother,' one of the men yelled over a speaker, even though I was standing only 17 steps away from him.

My mom talked to the men. 'Don't yell at him. You'll scare him even more.' She paused for a second. 'Let me through. We found him. Oh God, we really found him. You have to let me through! He's my son and he can't handle you yelling at him!'

Then she talked to me again, across the front yard. 'It's going to be okay, honey. We will get those socks off you in no time. These men are here to help you. They're going to bring you to me.'

I could feel them walking closer. My heart felt like it was going to beat out of my chest. I counted my heartbeats until I got to 149. I could hear their breathing against their helmets as they got right near me. I tried to count their breaths, but I kept seeing the glint of the lights off their guns instead. I closed my eyes and squatted down fast, covering my ears with my hands. I needed my momma.

'Mommmmma!' I yelled one last time before it all went white.

I opened my eyes to a ceiling full of square tiles this time. I didn't know where I was, but I wasn't at

Uncle Dan's. He didn't have square tiles on his ceiling. I counted up to 63 before I heard my momma say my name. 'Pepper?'

I looked over and saw her sweet face. It made me catch my breath. I had forgotten how she looked. I had forgotten that one of her eyes was bigger than the other and that she had lips that she had always thought were fat. I had forgotten her perfect eyebrows and the way her cheeks crinkled into dimples when she smiled. I had missed how white her teeth were, and her silver cross necklace that was still hanging around her neck. I started to cry, because I had forgotten so much of her. My mind was supposed to remember her, every little piece of her, but I had forgotten.

'Pepper, don't cry. It's all right.' She hesitated for a minute and got her worried lines on her forehead. I wanted to reach up and smooth them out so they didn't stick there forever. She sat on the bed and held my hand. Her hand was warm and covered mine up. Her fingernails looked like she had been biting them again, and the skin around was ragged too. 'You okay?'

I looked around the room. I was in a metal bed with white sheets. Almost everything in the room was white. There was a beeping noise coming from a machine next to the bed. I started a running count of the beeps while I took in the room. I jumped when I saw a needle going into my hand, held in place by some white tape, with a tube that ran up, up, up to a bag of clear liquid. I knew that needles hurt. I had had shots at the doctor's office. That clear stuff was going into me, but it didn't hurt. The room smelled like the stuff they mopped the floor with at school.

'You're safe now. You're in a hospital. They're going to check you over and make sure you're okay.' She pointed to my arm. 'You were a little dehydrated, so they're giving you some fluids through that tube. You'll feel better really soon.'

I wiped my tears on the sheets, because I didn't want her to think I was a baby anymore. I wasn't ready to talk yet, but I liked hearing her voice again. I looked at her outfit to see if it was a yoga or a soccer day. She had on a skirt and a tank top with a pink short-sleeved sweater over it. It had seven white buttons down the front. I counted them without even thinking about it. I guess she wasn't going to yoga or soccer. I wasn't sure what she was doing today.

'That man isn't going to hurt you anymore. I'm here. And I'm going to stay with you always.'

I felt my eyes leak again, and I wanted to talk to her. I thought hard about what I wanted to say so that I could get the words just right. I wanted to tell her how much I had missed her. I wanted her to know that I had spent almost all of my time trying to figure out her numbers and trying hard in school, even though it was loud and the kids didn't really seem to want to hang out with me. I wanted her to know that I had learned all about chickens and how to drive a boat. I wanted her to know about

Ms. Harrison, and how she was really nice to me. How she was my only friend. It was all too much to tell her, though. So, I just started at the beginning, at That Amazing Pizza Place.

'I'm sorry, Momma. I let go of Rosalind Jane's hand. I went up in the tunnel. I just couldn't stand all of the loud noises. It was so loud in there. It hurt my ears, Momma. I'm so, so sorry. I missed you so much, like every single day, at school and at Uncle Dan's.'

'Uncle Dan?' she asked, her mouth made a little 'O' when she asked the question and her eyebrows bunched together like she didn't know what I was talking about. And in that second, I knew for sure that everything he had told me was a lie. She wasn't in heaven and she clearly wasn't dead. 'Baby, it's okay. You don't have to apologize. It wasn't your fault, Pepper. But you have to know that you're safe now.'

I smiled a little at that. 'You found me. I knew you would find me.' I stopped a second to remember. 'I know the name of the town, Momma. I remembered it. It's A-R-T-H-U-R-S-V-I-L-L-E. Arthursville. It's really long, but Ms. Harrison told me and I saw the letters in my brain like you told me to. I memorized them so you could find me. Actually I turned them into numbers so that they were easier to remember.'

'You did really good, Pepper. You're the smartest, bravest boy I know. Ms. Harrison helped us find you. When you called me on her phone, the police traced it to Arthursville, and then to Ms. Harrison at your school. At first she was scared, because she thought she had done something wrong. But she hadn't. She was nice to you, wasn't she?'

I nodded. I wondered if I would ever see Ms. Harrison again.

'She told me so much about the time she spent with you. How good you've done in school. How you still love Angry Birds and are a whiz at math. She told me how you surprised your teacher by doing the hardest math problems in your head, without even writing them down. Ms. Harrison really is your friend. She told the police about the time that you ran away from her.'

'Is she mad about me using her phone to call you? When I ran away from her, she got her mad voice on.' I cried a little bit more thinking about how she was so mad at me that day. I wiped away the tears really fast. Maybe Momma wouldn't notice. I didn't want to be a cry baby, but they kept leaking out of my eyes when I got upset.

'No, honey. She's not mad at you. She's happy that you found me. And that you're safe. She didn't even know that you were looking for me, but, because you are so smart, you figured it out. Now stop crying. Everybody's happy that you're safe.'

I wasn't sure what 'safe' meant. Wasn't I safe at Uncle Dan's? I felt safe except for the time that the fish splashed blood all over me.

'Where's Uncle Dan?'

'Hmmmmm. Uncle Dan? Is that what he told you? That he was your uncle?'

'He has a gold tooth just like you and he taught me how to fish. After six beers, he takes a nap. That's how I called you the first time.'

'He's gone away, Pepper. And he's not your uncle. He's not going to hurt you anymore.'

I felt a little bit sorry for Uncle Dan. 'He didn't hurt me, Momma. Well, only that once when I spilled ice cream all over his truck. Then I had a big goose egg on my forehead. He said it was because I took my seatbelt off and then the car in front of him stopped really fast. But I never take my seatbelt off until you tell me, or he told me. I was good about leaving my seatbelt on, even though he didn't have a booster seat. He let me sit in the front seat of his truck, but I think that was because there wasn't a back seat.'

Her eyes got big and she touched my forehead with her hand, even though the goose egg was long gone. 'Oh, baby. I'm so sorry.'

I took a deep breath. I had so much to tell her that the words kept running together. 'You don't have to be sorry. I know that if you had been there, then you would have stuck out your arm and saved me. Or I would have been in the back seat and it wouldn't have happened at all. But it wasn't your fault. I know you were looking for me the whole time.'

'I was. Did he hurt you in any other way, Pepper? You know how we talked about private parts of your body?'

I frowned. Uncle Dan never did anything like that. 'No, Momma. He didn't do that. He only hit me that one time, and it was because I kept screaming your name over and over in the truck. Mostly he was nice to me. He zipped me into his jacket one time when it was too loud at school. He made me pancakes and bacon. He didn't make me eat his eggs or toast with butter. I hate butter. And he showed me how to feed the chickens and how not to get bit by the rooster. I didn't like the rooster very much.' I stopped for a second. 'I got to gather up the eggs every morning. Did you know that chickens sometimes lay brown eggs, or white eggs, but other times they are kind of pink or purple? I didn't like the ones that had blood on them, but Uncle Dan said they just needed washing.' I stopped again. I hadn't talked so much in so long. It was hard to get my brain to make all the right words.

'We'll get the doctor to look at your head and make sure you're okay, sweetie. You're going to be fine, but we will just have them check your head one more time.'

'It doesn't hurt at all anymore. It was a long time ago, in the truck. After he saved me in the ball pit at That Amazing Pizza Place. After about a week, it went down and then I had these big purple circles around my eyes. But they went away after another week.'

She frowned at my answer, but I wasn't sure why.

'Momma, can I ask you something?'

'Sure, baby. Anything. You hungry or cold? You need something to drink? Or do you want to watch tv?'

'No, I'm okay. Maybe something to eat in a little bit if they have bacon here.'

She smiled. 'We will get you bacon, Pepper. No matter what. Now what did you want to ask me?'

'Why isn't Uncle Dan my uncle anymore? How come they took him?'

She cried when I said that, and pulled me close to her. I breathed her in; her vanilla made me cry more too. I had missed her vanilla so much. I had missed her so much. All along I just knew I would get back to her and her face and her smell. I was finally home again. I survived.

There are things I know, things I remember, and things that other people tell me. But nobody had to tell me how my momma smelled, how home smelled. That was one thing that I never forgot.

Acknowledgements

This book would not be possible without the valuable help from Neal Mynatt, who painstakingly reviewed draft after draft of each scene. Thank you also to the folks at Fairlight Books for believing in me. And my parents, who have engrained in me the courage to take a shot.

FAIRLIGHT MODERNS

Bookclub and writers' circle notes for all the
Fairlight Moderns can be found at
www.fairlightmoderns.com

SOPHIE VAN LLEWYN

Bottled Goods

When Alina's brother-in-law defects to the West, she and her husband become persons of interest to the secret services, causing both of their careers to come grinding to a halt. As the strain takes its toll on their marriage, Alina turns to her aunt for help – the wife of a communist leader, and a secret practitioner of the old folk ways.

Set in 1970s communist Romania, this novella-in-flash draws upon magic realism to weave a tale of everyday troubles that can't be put down.

'It is a story to savour, to smile at, to rage against and to weep over.'
- Zoe Gilbert, author of *FOLK*

'Sophie van Llewyn has brought light into an era which cast a long shadow.'
- Joanna Campbell, author of *Tying Down the Lion*

SARA MARCHANT

The Driveway Has Two Sides

On an East Coast island, full of tall pine moaning with sea gusts, Delilah moves into a cottage by the shore. The locals gossip as they watch her clean, black hair tied back in a white rubber band. They don't like it when she plants a garden out front – orange-red *Carpinus caroliniana* and silvery blue hosta. Very unusual, they whisper. Across the driveway lives a man who never goes out. Delilah knows he's watching her and she likes the look of him, but perhaps life's too complicated already...

'This devourable novella is one part Barbara Pym, one part Patricia Highsmith and all parts Sara Marchant.'
— Jill Alexander Essbaum, author
of *Hausfrau*

EMMA TIMPANY

Travelling in the Dark

Sarah is travelling with her young son back to her home town in the South of New Zealand. When debris from an earthquake closes the road before her, she is forced to extend her journey, and divert through the places from her youth that she had hoped never to return to. As the memories of her childhood resurface, she knows that for the sake of her son, she must face up to them now or be lost forever.

'A tour de force of imagery and emotion.'
- Clio Gray, author of *The Anatomist's Dream*

ANTHONY FERNER

Inside the Bone Box

*"As he tiptoed his way through the twisting paths
of sulci and fissures and ventricles, he'd play
Bach, something austere yet dynamic."*

Nicholas Anderton is a highly respected neurosurgeon
at the top of his field. But behind the successful façade
all is not well. Tormented by a toxic marriage, and
haunted by past mistakes, Anderton has been eating
to forget. His wife, meanwhile, has turned to drink.

There are sniggers behind closed doors – how can a
surgeon be fat, they whisper; when mistakes are made
and his old adversary Nash steps in to take advantage
Anderton knows things are coming to a head...

Anthony Ferner is a former professor of
international business and is published widely
in non-fiction in his field. He has one other
published novella, *Winegarden*.